WRITE
MURDER DOWN

Write
Murder Down

RICHARD LOCKRIDGE

J. B. LIPPINCOTT COMPANY
Philadelphia and New York

For HILDY

1

They walked down Sixth Avenue from Charles Restaurant. It was the longest day of the year and, although they had not hurried over dinner, there was a glow almost of sunset when they crossed Tenth Street and looked west. It was a warm evening, not a hot one. The air was, uncharacteristically, breathable. She wore a sleeveless yellow dress with a dark green belt and her black hair fell almost to her shoulders. With heels, she was as tall as he, or almost. It was a fine evening, Anthony Cook thought, and for once no telephone call had interrupted it. So far, of course. It was an evening, Tony Cook told himself, during which there wouldn't be any telephone call.

They walked past the library which had been a courthouse and past the tall, angular building which had been a jail. They turned into Christopher Street. Rachel Farmer said, "Who was the beard?"

It pulled Tony Cook back from warming thoughts of other things. He said, "What?" Then he said, "What beard?"

"The red one," Rachel said. "At the bar. Not that I remember all that many beards. The one who—"

"Oh," Tony said. "That one."

"That one," Rachel agreed. "Not that it matters."

They had been sitting at the Charles bar, which is a rec-

1

tangle. They had got the last two bar stools with backs on them, which are favored by those who favor the bar of Charles French Restaurant. Across the rectangle, beyond the bottles and the glasses and the moving bartenders, the stools do not have backs. You can, of course, tilt against the wall, but then you have to reach out for your drink.

"We're in luck," Tony said, when they found their stools at a little after six. The bartender said, "Evening, folks. The usual?" Rachel said, "Lady luck is sitting beside us, Tony," and Tony Cook said "Yes" to both of them. He thought, she doesn't call me "Mister" any more, the way she did at first. The bartender filled a stemmed glass with crushed ice and put cubes into a squat glass and measured Old Fitzgerald over the cubes. He emptied the crushed ice from the stemmed glass and poured chilled Tio Pepe into it. They touched glasses and put them down on the bar, and the bartender put a dish of mixed nuts between them.

A man with a red beard around the corner of the bar looked at them and smiled through his beard. It was a well-groomed beard and very red. Then, when he saw that they were looking at him, he raised his glass.

Tony lifted his glass, returning a salute. After a moment's hesitation, Rachel lifted hers. They both smiled across their drinks at the man with the red beard.

And that was all of it. They finished their drinks and Tony nodded his head for the bartender, but the headwaiter came to say, "I have a table in the café now, sir-madame. I will bring your drinks, yes?"

The man with the red beard was talking to the man on the stool next to his. They were led to a table in a recess, and shared it with an opulent nude in a heavy gilt frame. Rachel looked at the nude and said, "Representational," and Tony said, "Very," and they finished their drinks and decided against others—"When we get home," Rachel said, "if we want them"—and ordered dinner.

"Anyway," Tony said when they were sipping coffee, "they didn't redo the kitchen."

They had walked south on Sixth Avenue, not hurrying. The

2

evening relaxed around them. They turned from Christopher into Gay Street, which is narrow and has a twist in it.

"A client?" Rachel said. "The beard, I mean?"

"No," Tony said. "A man who lives in the same building I do. On the top floor. We—oh, run into each other on the stairs. That sort of thing. His name's Shepley. Shepherd. Something like that. We just—"

He stopped because Rachel was not, he thought, listening. She hesitated and looked up at the building they were in front of. He looked where she seemed to be looking and looked at a second-story window with no light behind it. They walked on, around the twist, and Rachel said, "I guess she's finished." Tony said, "Did she have a red beard?" and they both laughed, and climbed the steps to the front door of the narrow old building in which Rachel lived.

"For weeks," Rachel said, as she got the key out of her handbag, "she's been sitting at that window—open most of the time—pounding a typewriter. Almost every evening. Not that I go by every evening, of course. When I do. Sometimes it's been midnight. With a light behind her, falling on the typewriter. So that she's—oh, just a silhouette."

She turned the key in the vestibule lock and he pulled the door open. They climbed a flight of familiar stairs, and she turned the key in another lock and went ahead of him into a living room, which was the width of the narrow house and had a lamp glowing in it for their return.

"I just sort of wondered about her," Rachel said. "She always seemed to—oh, so intent."

"Probably just a typist working overtime," Tony said, and she turned to face him. He held out his arms to her and she moved into them. They held each other tightly. Then she drew away and said, "This is a new dress. We mustn't muss it up."

"That can be prevented," Tony said and she laughed a little in her throat and said, "Yes, Tony," and walked away from him and opened the door to the bedroom. She partly closed the door behind her.

Tony Cook took off his summer jacket and unbuckled the

3

shoulder holster which held the .32-caliber Smith & Wesson which he could wear off duty instead of the heavier gun. He put the holstered revolver on a chair and laid his coat over it and made sure the outer door was locked. The department does not approve of men who leave weapons exposed to greedy hands.

He went through the bedroom door.

She was slender and tall and naked as she stood facing him.

"You've still got your clothes on," Rachel Farmer said and there was the mimicry of protest in her voice.

"That can be remedied," Tony Cook said, and his fingers went up to his necktie, which was a place to start.

She threw back the covers on the bed and, when he was ready, stood in front of him again, and they put their arms around each other. It was what Tony had been thinking about for some hours; it was what his warm thoughts had been about.

Without her heels, she was not as tall as he was. But they had measured their lengths before.

It was a little before midnight when he buckled his Smith & Wesson on again, reluctantly and at her insistence. "You've got the eight-to-four," she told him, "and I'm supposed to start posing at ten. I hope it keeps on being warm because Mackenowitz's place lets the air in everywhere. I freeze in winter. Good night, Tony. Go home, Tony."

He went down the flight of stairs and made sure the door at the bottom was locked after him. He went along Gay Street toward Christopher. Around the twist he looked up at the window Rachel had looked up at. There was no light behind it. He thought it was closed. When I was a boy, he thought, you could hardly walk through a street in the Village without hearing the click of typewriter keys through open windows. It isn't that way any more. On the third floor of the last house he passed in Gay Street they were having a party. It was a pretty noisy party. On a step of a stoop in Christopher Street a young man with long hair was sitting, doing nothing and seeming to be looking at nothing. I must have been in my early teens, Tony Cook thought, when I was walking through Mor-

4

ton Street and there was a young man of about the same age sitting on a stoop. I didn't say anything to him but he said, "I'm writing a poem. Go away." So I went away.

Perhaps the woman in Gay Street Rachel looked up at was writing a poem. It would have had to be a long poem. But perhaps people don't write poems on typewriters. It's not anything I know about. What I know about is being a cop. What I know about is evenings like this and Rachel. I can't write poems about evenings like this—evenings when the telephone doesn't ring.

In the vestibule of the converted house he lived in on Twelfth Street, he remembered the man with the red beard and looked under the top-floor bell push for a name. He had been right about the name—right the first time, anyway. "Laurence Shepley." That was the name of the beard; the name of the man he had passed once or twice on the stairs and who had raised his glass to them at the Charles bar.

He went up the stairs to his own apartment on the second floor. He set the alarm clock for seven, which would give him time to have breakfast and walk up to West Twentieth Street. If the weather held.

It's been a fine evening, he thought as he was ending it in sleep. Evenings with her always make fine evenings. If the telephone doesn't ring.

2

He had a report to write; he always had reports to write in the prescribed stiffness of departmental prose. Detectives spend a lot of their time writing reports, and that morning's was one of the dullest. It should have been a routine affair for precinct; the "brain boys" of Homicide, Manhattan South, shouldn't have been called in on it. A man had come home drunk in the middle of the afternoon and started slapping his wife around, for no apparent reason, and had slapped too hard in the wrong place and she had died of it. Which precinct had wrapped up before he and Detective (2nd gr.) Tompkins had got there.

Yesterday was a dull day, Detective (1st gr.) Anthony Cook thought, and completed his report and put it in channels. Dull until six in the evening. Today looked like being as dull, he thought, tilting back his chair in the squad room. And there wouldn't be any six o'clock reprieve. Not on this Friday, the twenty-third of June. After a morning posing for Mackenowitz, in a studio which shouldn't be too drafty on a day like this, she had an afternoon in front of cameras and under glaring lights.

"They'll be at it until God knows when, Tony," she had told him. "Until I fall apart at the seams, probably."

6

He had told her that she never would and that, all right, they'd make it Saturday.

He lighted a cigarette and waited. At about a quarter of eleven he began to wonder whether the people of the City of New York weren't killing one another any more. At a quarter after eleven the telephone on his desk rang, in the harsh and abrupt way of telephones.

He wasn't catching for the squad, but it might be an outside call anyway. He said, "Homicide South, Detective Cook."

The voice which answered him was mournful. It was dispirited. Tony didn't need identification, but he got it. He said, "Be right along, Lieutenant," and went out of the squad room and a short way along a corridor. The door of Detective Lieutenant Nathan Shapiro's small, hot office was partly open, and Tony went in and closed the door behind him. Shapiro looked at him through mournful eyes. Tony Cook said, "Good morning, Nate," because Nathan Shapiro disliked to be addressed in formal terms when there weren't civilians around. Lieutenant Shapiro has an abiding certainty that his rank is somebody's astonishing mistake and will one day prove a disaster to the New York Police Department.

"Down in the Village," Shapiro said, in his usual hopeless tone, "some woman's killed herself. Only now precinct thinks maybe she hasn't. Because they can't find any barbiturates in her apartment, and she was full of some barbiturate. So the chief's told Bill we'd better rally round. Here."

Tony Cook had sat down on the chair across from Shapiro at Shapiro's desk. Nathan Shapiro pushed an autopsy report across the desk to him.

Unidentified female. Age late twenties or early thirties. Dead approximately thirty-six hours at the time of the post-mortem examination. Cause of death, loss of blood. Toxicological analysis showed a massive dose of a barbiturate prior to death.

"Cleaning woman found her," Shapiro said. "About eight this morning. In the bathtub in this Gay Street apart—"

He stopped because Tony Cook stood up—stood up so sud-

7

denly that the chair he had been sitting on fell backward and clattered on the floor.

Tony said, *"Gay Street,"* and the words came out in a kind of gasp.

Nathan Shapiro's long sad face was broken by a smile. He shook his head.

"No, Tony," Shapiro said. "I wouldn't have thrown it at you that way. Two or three doors from Miss Farmer's apartment."

Tony Cook said, "Sorry," and pulled the chair up from the floor and sat down on it. He looked again at the autopsy report, which went on for some paragraphs. "Dead approximately thirty-six hours." When you're jumpy, you can forget the obvious. Tony said, again, "I'm sorry, Nate."

"In a bathtub," Shapiro said. "She'd cut her wrists. Or, anyway, her wrists were cut and she bled to death. Knife—ordinary paring knife—in the tub with the body. Sometimes they take barbiturates before they slash themselves. Cut their wrists to hurry things up, I suppose. Only—no barbiturate in the apartment. Come to that, there was damn little of anything in the apartment. Oh, a dress in a closet. Things to go under the dress. A pair of shoes."

"Just one dress?"

"From what precinct says. Detective named—" Shapiro looked at a notepad on his desk. "Detective named Pieronelli. From Charles Street."

"Charles Pieronelli," Tony said. "I've worked with him. Matter of fact, we both have. Remember?"

"I don't—" Shapiro said and caught himself and said, "Yes. On that evangelist kill." He sighed. "I'm losing my memory," he said. "Comes on you with age, I suppose."

Tony looked across the desk at Nathan Shapiro. He tried to keep his smile from turning into laughter. He said, "Sure," in as grave a voice as he could manage. He knew that Shapiro was in his early forties, so the agreement wasn't as gravely phrased as he wanted it to be. And after a moment, Nathan Shapiro smiled back at him. The smile changed his mournful face considerably.

8

"But after all," Tony said, "you're still pretty good with a gun. You admit that yourself."

"I talk too much," Shapiro said. "All right, let's get going. Way Bill Weigand wants it. Says you know the Village better than most." He paused for a moment. "Gay Street particularly, Bill says."

"Everybody knows everything," Tony said. "Comes of being a cop and having to leave telephone numbers even when you're off duty."

Shapiro nodded his head. He said, "Well, we asked for it, Tony," and stood up behind his desk. Tony followed Lieutenant Shapiro out of the hot little office and along the corridor and down the stairs and into the unmarked sedan waiting for them in the street. It did not take them long to get to the Charles Street station and into one of the inquiry rooms. It was a bleak room with a table and a few stiff chairs. Pieronelli was sitting on a chair on one side of the table. A rather heavy Negro woman was sitting on a chair on the other side of the table. Cook said, "Morning, Charley," and Pieronelli said, "Hi, Tony. Morning, Lieutenant. This is Mrs. Jenkinson. She found the body."

"That poor Miss Jones," Mrs. Jenkinson said. "Such a nice lady. To do that to herself."

"Mrs. Jenkinson got to the apartment about eight o'clock this morning," Pieronelli said. "Went in Tuesday and Friday mornings to straighten the place up. An hour or two at a time. Didn't expect to see this Miss Jones. Almost never did see her. That's right, Mrs. Jenkinson?"

"No almost about it," Mrs. Jenkinson said, firmly. "Never did see her except that once, about a month ago, when we made the arrangements and she gave me the key. Way I understood it, she went to the apartment in the afternoons. She was a nice lady. She'd leave my money for me Fridays. More than I really had coming, sometimes. She was a nice lady."

"You only saw her that once?" Shapiro asked her.

"Just that once," Mrs. Jenkinson said. "You a policeman too, mister?"

"Yes," Shapiro said. "Did she sleep in the apartment? I

mean, you went in about eight in the mornings and she wasn't there. Had her bed been slept in?"

"Not most of the time. When it had I made it up for her. But that was only two or three times since I started working for her. Sometimes I thought—well, there wasn't really enough for me to do for what she paid me. And I likes to do the work I gets paid for."

"I'm sure you do," Shapiro said. "What did you do, Mrs. Jenkinson? Besides making the bed the few times she'd used it?"

"Went over the floors with a dry mop. Swept them skimpy rag rugs—what you gets in these furnished apartments. Did the bathroom. First time I sort of straightened up her papers but the next time there was a note saying please would I not touch the papers. So after that I didn't."

"What kind of papers were they?"

"Papers with typing on them. Beside her typewriter."

"Typewriter?" Tony Cook said. "Was her typewriter by one of the street windows, Mrs. Jenkinson?"

"Yes," Mrs. Jenkinson said. "So she could get the light, I guess. Only, it wasn't there this morning. Anyway, I don't think it was. Finding her—finding her that way—well, things sort of went out of my mind. I—I just I just went sort of faint like. It—it was an awful thing to see, mister."

"I'm sure it was," Shapiro said. "And I know you've already told about it to Detective Pieronelli here. Probably to others. But I'll have to ask you to go over it again, I'm afraid. About finding Miss—her name was Jones, you say?"

"That's what she told me, anyway."

"Yes. Miss Jones's body in the bathtub?"

"It was awful. There was water in the tub and it was—was all red."

"I know," Shapiro said. "You went to the apartment about eight o'clock this morning and used your key to let yourself in. Go ahead from there, will you, Mrs. Jenkinson?"

"Usually when I goes into the apartments of ladies I work for I say good morning," Mrs. Jenkinson said. "Only at Miss Jones's I didn't, on account of she wouldn't be there. I

10

just went in. I decided I might as well start in the bedroom and make up the bed, if it needed making up."

She paused and looked at Shapiro, a question in her broad dark face.

"Yes," Shapiro said. "That's what I want to hear about. Go ahead, Mrs. Jenkinson. The bed?"

The bed had not been slept in. She went on into the bathroom, carrying fresh towels. "I always gave her fresh towels on Friday."

Her employer—"the lady"—was lying in the bathtub. The tub was almost full of reddened water. "I said, 'Miss Jones? Miss Jones, honey,' but I knew she couldn't hear me. Then I went all faint like for a minute or two. Then I got out to the telephone. It was in the living room and I got the operator and said something awful had happened and that I wanted to talk to the police. And then I sat down in a chair, because I felt faint like, and pretty soon the police came. And then a lot of other people. And after while Mr. Pieronelli and another man. And then they brought me down here and I told them about it."

"Yes," Shapiro said. "When you saw her in the bathtub was she wearing anything?"

"A nightgown. Sort of—oh, thin, if you know what I mean. The kind you can almost see through. Only—only it was all red, like everything else."

"Was there much water in the tub, Mrs. Jenkinson?"

"It was pretty near full, I guess. But her head wasn't in the water. It was sort of propped back against the tub."

Shapiro said he saw. He said, "Was the water running? Into the tub, I mean?"

"I don't know, sir. It—it was such an awful thing that I got all faint like. Could be it was only—only I don't remember hearing water running."

Shapiro looked at Pieronelli.

"Not when we got there," Pieronelli said. "I doubt if any of the boys would have turned it off. Unless it was overflowing, of course. No prints on the faucet, the boys say."

"The water?"

"Almost up to the overflow outlet. Full of blood. Cold when we got there. But—all right—so was she. You've seen the autopsy report, Lieutenant. Dead about thirty-six hours when they got to her. They cool off when they've been dead that long."

Shapiro said, "Thanks, Pieronelli." Pieronelli said, "Sorry, sir." Shapiro turned back to Mrs. Jenkinson.

"Just Miss Jones?" he said. "Didn't tell you her first name?"

"No, mister."

"She didn't leave your money in a check?"

"No. Just the money. Sometimes more, maybe a dollar more, than it came to by rights."

Shapiro turned back to Detective Pieronelli and raised his eyebrows.

"Unlisted number," Pieronelli said. "Subscriber just 'A. Jones.' Installed three weeks ago, the company says."

"The man who installed it?"

"We haven't got to him yet, Lieutenant. The company's checking for us. Says it is, anyway. Says it may take a while."

"Let's hope they don't get a wrong number," Nathan Shapiro said.

"No barbiturates in the apartment?"

"Not that Bob Holmes and I could find. Holmes will go over it again when the fingerprint boys finish. Nothing in the medicine cabinet in the bathroom, anyway."

"You mean no bottle of barbiturate tablets?"

"I mean not a damn thing, sir. No toothpaste and no toothbrush. None of the things women put on their faces. Just nothing at all."

"No typewriter? No papers with typing on them?"

"No, Lieutenant. Just a white dress in a closet on a hanger. And a bra and what they call pantyhose. Oh, yes, and a pair of white shoes. Sandals, that is—summery, like the dress. Except for that—the dress and things, I mean—you wouldn't have thought anybody was living in the apartment. Come to that, there wasn't anybody when we got there. Living there, I mean."

"Yes," Shapiro said, "I know what you mean. Mrs. Jenkinson,

12

you're quite sure there was a typewriter? Except this morning, I mean? On a table by the window?"

"Course I am. You think I'm lying to you, man?"

"No," Shapiro said. "A typewriter and a pile of paper beside it. With typing on the paper, you say?"

"First time I was there. Like I said, I straightened the papers up a little. Made them neat, sort of. That was before she left me the note saying not to."

Shapiro said, "Yes, Tony?"

Anthony Cook hadn't said anything. He had merely moved a little. For a man who was good only with a gun, Tony thought, Nathan Shapiro was extremely observant.

"We're going over there?" Cook said and Shapiro said, "Of course, Tony."

"Because," Tony Cook said, "there's something I can maybe help check out. If it's the place I think it is."

"All right," Shapiro said. "See that Mrs. Jenkinson gets home all right, will you, Pieronelli?"

Pieronelli said, "Sure." Mrs. Jenkinson said, "I got two more ladies to do for. Only by now maybe they think I've stood them up. Two ladies and a gentleman, if I can get to him."

"I'll see that she gets where she wants to go," Pieronelli said, and Shapiro and Tony Cook went out to the unmarked sedan and drove the few blocks to Gay Street. There were two cruise cars and the lab truck in Gay Street, parked partly on the sidewalk. Somebody could get past them in a car if he didn't mind going up on the other sidewalk. Gay Street is not a wide street. Tony parked the car, partly on the sidewalk, behind the lab truck.

Shapiro started to climb the few gritty steps which led up to the front door of the narrow house. Tony stood on the sidewalk and looked up at the house, and Shapiro said, "You coming along, Tony?"

"I'm pretty sure it's the same house," Tony said. "Same window Rach—Miss Farmer looked up at last night. In fact, I'm damn sure."

Shapiro came back down the steps and joined Cook in look-

13

ing up at the window. It was one of two windows on the second floor.

"For a couple of weeks, Miss Farmer says, there's been a woman sitting near that window—most of the time with it open—pounding on a typewriter. In the evenings. Sometimes late at night, I gathered. We—well, we happened to be walking by here last night and Rach—I mean Miss Farmer—said she guessed the woman was finished."

"You can call Miss Farmer Rachel," Shapiro said. "After all, you brought her over to see us once. Said she guessed the woman was finished?"

"With what she was doing," Tony said. "With whatever she was typing. That's all Rachel meant, Nate."

"Of course," Shapiro said. "She wasn't there last night? You're sure it's the right window? The one on the left?"

"Pretty sure," Tony said. "All right, I am sure. I checked it last night on my way home. It was dark then. And closed, I think."

"Let's go on up," Nathan Shapiro said, and led the way on up.

The door of the apartment at the top of the first flight of stairs was open. A uniformed patrolman stood outside it. Inside, two men were shaking dust on the little furniture there was in the room and blowing the dust off again. Another man with a small camera was taking pictures of surfaces from which they had blown the dust. A fourth man was standing watching them. He said, "Hello, Tony," and Tony said, "Hi, Bob," and, "This is Lieutenant Shapiro." The fourth man, who was broad-shouldered and heavy and had sandy hair, said, "Sir." Then he said, "They're about through, Lieutenant."

"And not getting much except hers," one of the fingerprint men said. "Hers clear enough all over. Somebody else's on the phone. Hers on the coffee cup, which was over there."

He pointed to a low, oblong table in front of a sofa which looked too hard to sit on.

"The boys took it away."

"Yes," Shapiro said. "Only one cup?"

"More in the kitchen on hooks in a cupboard. Only one on

14

the table. Three cups, two dinner plates, a little stainless steel stuff. No prints on any of it."

"I guess that does it," the man with the camera said. "A few that came up all right. Probably the deceased's. The ones on the phone. The rest pretty much blurs."

"The ones on the telephone probably are the cleaning woman's," Shapiro said.

The telephone rang. Shapiro raised his eyebrows at one of the fingerprint men and got a "Sure, Lieutenant" and picked the telephone up. He said his name into it. Then he listened. He said, "Thanks, Sergeant," and put it back in its cradle.

"There'd been coffee in the cup," he said. "Black. No cream or sugar. And a trace of Nembutal. Might have been almost a gram of the stuff in the coffee, they figure."

The fingerprint men were packing up. One of them said, "All yours, Lieutenant," and the three of them went out of the apartment and down the stairs.

"We may as well go over it again," Shapiro said, his voice sad. "Not that we'll find anything, probably."

The living room was, like Rachel's, the width of the narrow house. A narrower bedroom opened off it—a bedroom narrow and long, with a double bed occupying most of it. A bathroom opened off it and, nearer the front of the apartment, a tiny kitchen with a two-burner electric plate on top of a small refrigerator. In the kitchen there was a cabinet against one wall. Three coffee cups hung on hooks in the cabinet and two plates were on the shelf under them. In a drawer under the cabinet were two stainless steel knives and two forks to match them and a small jar of instant coffee. It was a little less than half full. There was a teaspoon beside the little jar.

Shapiro opened the refrigerator door, and it began to hum at him. It was empty. It looked, Nathan Shapiro thought, as if it had always been empty. As, he thought, does the whole apartment. It looks as if nobody had ever lived here. He went back into the bedroom.

Tony Cook had opened up the bed.

"Clean sheets," he said. "Don't look as if anybody'd ever slept on them. Clean pillow cases, too. The lab boys will have

15

run a vacuum over everything, of course. Looking for hairs and things."

Shapiro said, "Yes, Tony."

Detective Holmes came out of the bathroom. Looked at, he shrugged his shoulders. He said, "Not a thing, Lieutenant. Tub will need scrubbing out. Nothing in the—"

He stopped because Tony Cook, who had continued to look down at the bed as if it were hiding something, suddenly crouched and looked under it. He reached under it and lay on the floor and reached farther. He said, "Got it," and wriggled out and stood up.

He held "it" out to Shapiro. It was a key on a metal tag, and embossed on the tag were the words, "Hotel Algonquin, New York." Above the identifying words, punched into the metal, were numbers—"912."

Holmes said he'd be damned. He said, "Don't see how we missed it the first time around."

"Probably she stowed it under one of the pillows," Shapiro said. "Fell down between the end of the mattress and the headboard."

"Hell of a place to keep a key," Tony Cook said. "It's dusty. Mrs. Jenkinson didn't clean under beds very carefully."

"Miss Jones probably thought it was lost," Shapiro said. "The hotel gave her another and she kept it in her handbag."

"Of which there isn't any," Tony said.

"There wasn't," Holmes said. "That we wouldn't have missed. Just this dress and some of those pantyhose and a pair of shoes in that little closet." He pointed to a narrow door between the kitchen and the bathroom doors. "No handbag."

Shapiro opened the narrow door and looked into a narrow closet, with a rod across it and three coat hangers hooked to the rod. There was nothing else in the closet.

"Guys from the lab took her things," Holmes said. "And the paring knife that was in the tub. Cheap knife. Rough wooden handle." And Shapiro closed the narrow door and said, "Yes, Holmes. Their job." Holmes said, "That's right, Lieutenant."

"Nothing else here," Shapiro said. "At least, I hope there isn't. Come on, Tony. Put a seal on it, will you, Holmes?"

Holmes said, "Sure will, Lieutenant," and Shapiro went out of the bedroom and through the living room—the living room in which Shapiro felt nobody had ever lived—and down the stairs to the street. On the sidewalk, Shapiro stopped and looked up at the two windows of the second-floor apartment. He said, "Did Miss Farmer get a good look at this woman, do you think?"

Tony Cook didn't think she had. He told Shapiro what Rachel had said—about the woman at the typewriter having been merely an outline against a light.

"All the same," Shapiro said, "she might remember more, under the new circumstances. I'd like to know what this Miss Jones looked like."

"There'll be shots."

"They don't look the same when they're dead," Shapiro said. "Do you suppose Miss Farmer'll be at home now?"

Tony didn't think so. He said she'd be working.

"Could you find her, d'you think? See if she can add anything."

Tony Cook said he could try.

"I'll take the car," Nathan Shapiro said. "Go up to the Algonquin and ask around. On Forty-fourth, isn't it?"

Tony said it was—on Forty-fourth just off Sixth.

"If you turn up anything, try to check with me there," Shapiro said. "Or at the office and leave word where you'll be. O.K.?"

Tony said, "O.K.," and Shapiro went to the car and Tony went the other way, around the twist in Gay Street. There was a chance Rachel might have come home for a breather between jobs. He didn't think it was much of a chance. He rang the doorbell several times. Rachel hadn't come home for a breather. Probably she was still standing in Mackenowitz's drafty studio.

Tony knew where the studio was. He had picked her up there once when she had finished posing. It had been an off day for him and a Saturday and they had driven up to the country in a hired car. It had been a pleasant day in midspring. It had been a fine day in the country. And a fine night.

3

Shapiro had to drive through Forty-fourth Street almost to Fifth Avenue before he found a spot to wedge the police car into. He used the telephone in the car to say where he was and to learn that there were no messages for him. He locked the car up to be sure that it would still be there when he went for it and walked back through Forty-fourth Street with sunshine part of the time on his long sad face. He was a tall man in a gray suit which could have done with pressing. It was a warm day, but he kept the suit jacket buttoned to cover the gun. He walked west with long strides.

He had heard about the Hotel Algonquin. Everybody has heard about the Algonquin. He had never been in it. He went into the hotel and it was cool inside. He walked beside an almost-head-high partition until he came to the desk, and he stood there for a moment with his back to it.

He looked on a large room with chairs and sofas and people on most of them. He watched a man in a white jacket carrying drinks to tables. He heard the sharp tinkle of bells and saw that each table in the room had its little bell. Beyond the room was a wide entrance to "Restaurant." A group of four men—three of them looking like Madison Avenue and the fourth fuzzy with beard and long hair—was standing just inside the entrance. A man in a dinner jacket came up to them and

18

nodded his head and smiled and led them into the restaurant.

Shapiro turned back to the desk and saw what he wanted and went to the telephone at the end of the desk. He lifted the telephone and heard, "Can I help you?" in a light female voice.

"Room Nine-twelve, please," Shapiro said, and got, "Just a moment, sir," and a repeated buzzing sound. After a number of buzzes, Shapiro got what he had expected—"I'm afraid Room Nine-twelve doesn't answer, sir." Shapiro said, "Thank you," and hung up and went back along the desk.

A tall man smiled at him and at the same time shook his head. He said, "Have you a reservation, sir? I'm afraid if you haven't we're—"

"I don't want a room," Shapiro said. "Have you a Miss—or perhaps Mrs.—A. Jones registered here?"

The reception clerk turned to a rack and flicked cards. He turned back and shook his head. He said, "A Mr. Armand Jones?"

"No," Shapiro said. He took the key marked "912" out of his pocket and put it on the desk. He also took his badge out of his pocket and put it beside the key. The clerk picked the badge up and looked at it. Then he looked at Shapiro. Then he said, "Yes, Lieutenant?"

"I'd like to know who's occupying Room Nine-twelve," Shapiro said. "He—or more likely she—doesn't answer the phone."

The man behind the desk said, "Well," drawing it out. Shapiro said, "Police business," and pointed at the badge still on the desk. He said, "I'll pin it on, if you'd rather. Where it shows."

"That won't be necessary," the clerk said. "That won't be at all necessary. Would you like to see the manager, Lieutenant?"

"All I want at the moment," Shapiro said, "is the name of whoever is occupying Room Nine-twelve."

The desk clerk looked doubtful. When he spoke it was with doubt in his voice. But what he said was, "Well, I guess so, Lieutenant."

He turned to another rack and flipped cards in it. He came

back to Shapiro. He said, "A Miss Lacey, Lieutenant. Miss Jo-An Lacey."

"Joan?"

"Two words, the way it's registered. 'Jo' dash 'An.' She's been with us for some weeks, Lieutenant. About a month, actually. Sir?"

The inquiring "Sir?" was not addressed to Nathan Shapiro. It was for a tall, youngish man with a neatly clipped but very thick red beard. It was followed by, "Can I help you?"

"Will you have Miss Lacey paged?" the red beard said. "Miss Jo-An Lacey? She doesn't seem to be in her room and I've looked in the Oak Room and the Rose Room and—anyway, we've got a lunch date. Perhaps she left a message?"

"I don't think so," the clerk said. "Who would the message be for?"

"Shepley. Laurence Shepley."

The tall desk clerk made a business of looking through a shelf under the desk. He stood up and shook his head. He said, "I'm afraid not, Mr. Shepley. Held up in traffic, probably. But I'll have her paged." Then he looked at Nathan Shapiro.

"We seem," Nathan said, "to be looking for the same person, Mr. Shepley. A friend of yours, this Miss Lacey?"

"Business of yours?" the man with the red beard said.

Nathan Shapiro reached for and picked up his badge. He cupped it in his hand and showed it to Laurence Shepley. Shepley looked at the badge. He said, "I don't get it, Lieutenant. Looking for Jo-An?"

"She is a friend of yours, then?"

"I know her. You don't read much, do you?"

Shapiro let surprise and bewilderment show in his long face. Then he said, "A reasonable amount. Why?"

"Her name doesn't ring a bell?"

Nathan Shapiro said he was afraid it didn't.

"Couple of years ago, three maybe, she wrote one hell of a novel. Called it *Snake Country*. A hell of a novel and a hell of a best seller. The movie wasn't so hot. Still no bell, Lieutenant?"

"No bell," Shapiro said. There was no point in saying that

20

there was a tinkle. Not the sharp tinkle of the bell on the hotel desk. The clerk said, "Leon. Page Miss Lacey. Miss Jo-An Lacey for this gentleman." He indicated the man with the red beard. And Shepley said, "Maybe you'd better forget it, Mr. Arthur."

"Yes," Nathan Shapiro said. "I'm afraid she won't answer, Mr. Shepley. Suppose we sit down somewhere and you can tell me what you know about Miss Lacey."

Shepley said, "I don't see—" and then, "Oh, all right." He walked into the lounge, which now was almost full. But people were getting up from chairs and sofas and greeting people who came in and then going with them into the restaurant. Shepley found a small table with a chair on either side of it. There was a bell on the table and Shepley tapped it. When nothing happened immediately he tapped it again, several times. A waiter appeared. He said, "Gentlemen?"

"Bourbon and plain water," Shepley said. "Old Crow if you've got it. Yours, Lieutenant?"

Shapiro hesitated for a moment, not especially because he was on duty. His stomach objects to spirits. "Sherry," Nathan Shapiro said. "Not too dry." The waiter said, "Gentlemen," and went away.

"About Miss Lacey?" Shapiro said.

"Suppose you tell me," Shepley said. "What's Jo-An got to do with the police? She's a damn sweet person, and if you're going to say you're after her for—"

"No," Shapiro said. "Not in the sense you mean. Have you known her long, Mr. Shepley?"

"Not very. Three weeks or so. We met at a shindig some publisher was throwing. We ran into each other and we were both bored as hell and—well, we went somewhere where we weren't bored. You may as well tell me, don't you think? Where the police come into whatever the police do come into."

Shapiro thought a moment. Then he said, "A young woman committed suicide down in the Village yesterday. Or the night before. Or, perhaps she didn't kill herself. In an apartment in Gay Street. She was, she'd told people, a Miss Jones. We're by no means certain yet, but there was a room key in her apartment. It was for Room Nine-twelve in this hotel. Miss Lacey is booked into that room. She's not in it now. Anyway, she's not answering her telephone. As you found out, too. We'd—say we'd like to talk to her."

The waiter brought their drinks. Shepley merely stared at his. Then he said, "Jesus!" He picked his glass up and put it down again without drinking from it. He looked hard across the table at Shapiro.

"As I said," Shapiro told him, "we want to talk to Miss Lacey. Ask her how her door key happened to be in this Gay Street place."

"That isn't really it, is it?" Shepley said. He picked up his glass and this time drank from it. He put it down on the table. He put it down hard. When he spoke, he spoke slowly, heavily.

"What you're getting at," Shepley said, "you think Jo-An was this Miss Jones. And that she's dead. That's what you think, isn't it?"

"We think it's possible," Shapiro said. "How well did you get to know Miss Lacey, Mr. Shepley? After this meeting at the party?"

"Not all that well," Shepley said. "I took her to dinner a couple of times. We had drinks at my place once. We—oh, we talked a lot. We were in the same—well, we both called it trade. We talked about that. I don't mean we were in the same class at it. Damn near nobody has ever heard of Laurence Shepley. Damn near everybody had heard of her. A 'New Voice from the South.' That sort of—well, that sort of crap. But all the same, she was good. A couple of early tries. Then *Snake Country* and—wham!"

"You talked about her work? And yours?"

"I told her *Snake Country* was damn good. Which she knew without my telling her. She'd never heard of anything I've done—a few short stories, but that market's pretty well dried up. Articles. Anything that will make a buck. You see, Lieutenant, I'm a pro. Getting by. She—well, she was a pro too.

22

Only—I keep using the past tense about her. You think that's the right tense, don't you?"

"I don't know, Mr. Shepley."

"You think probably."

"Yes, I'm afraid so."

"It'll be a damn shame if you're right. Because she was just finishing another book and thought it was going to be better than the snake-country thing."

"You and she just—oh, had drinks together? And dinners together? And talked."

"If you mean did we sleep together, hell, no. That didn't come into it. All right, I was a man and she was a woman and —well, a damn good-looking woman. But I've got a regular girl. We—Jo-An and I—we're just a couple of people in the same line of work. She way up and I just scrambling along. But the same line of work, all the same. We—well, we got sort of fond of each other in a mild sort of way. She was pretty much alone up here. Wanted somebody to talk to. Things happen that way, you know."

"Yes. You say 'voice from the South.' Where in the South, do you know?"

"Mobile, Alabama. Somewhere around Mobile, anyway. She talked like it, although not all that much like it."

"You say she's good-looking. Can you describe her to me?"

"Not the sort of thing I'm good at, Lieutenant. When I write fiction, which I don't often any more, I don't go into physical descriptions much. Give an outline. Let the readers fill it in. When there turn out to be readers, that is. Jo-An—oh, about five feet five. Brown hair to her shoulders. Brown eyes. Good figure. Rather high-pitched voice, like lots of Southern women. She dressed well. God knows she ought to have been able to, even with the lousy deal she got."

"Lousy deal?"

"Look, I said she was a pro. But all the same, she didn't really know her way around. We talked about that sort of thing, of course. It's a thing writers do talk about. Oh, a little about how you get your effects. But mostly about what you get out of them." He rubbed together the tips of the fingers of his right hand. He said, "Get what I mean, Lieutenant?"

"I guess so. This lousy deal?"

"You know anything about writers—writers and publishers and things like that?"

"Not much," Shapiro said, in a discouraged voice. He is always getting involved in matters of which he knows nothing. With painters and religious zealots and people of the theater —all things of which he knows nothing. He sighed and sipped from his glass of sherry. In spite of what he had asked for, it was dry. His stomach wouldn't approve.

"When she signed the contract for this first book of hers," Shepley said. "Years ago, that was. When she was just a kid. She signed the form the publisher gave her. The kind, years ago, most publishers just handed out. Straight ten per cent all the way through, believe it or not. Publisher got half of all subsidiary rights when he didn't get seventy-five. And an option on her next two on the same terms. *The same terms,* for God's sake!"

He drank deeply from his glass, almost finishing it. He shook his head. He said, again, "For God's sake."

Shapiro said, "Those aren't good terms, Mr. Shepley?"

Shepley looked across the table at him. He shook his head again. When he spoke again he spoke slowly and quietly, suiting his tone and words to the innocent.

"The sort of contract publishers don't try to get away with any more," he said. "Oh, the good ones never did. You know writers get royalties on their books, don't you? On the retail price, in most cases. Sometimes on the price the publisher gets from retailers and wholesale houses. But that's not the usual way. A book sells for—oh, five ninety-five, maybe, at the book store. At ten per cent, the writer gets fifty-nine and a half cents a book."

"I can," Shapiro said, "figure percentages."

"Some of the kids can't," Shepley said. "Kids like Jo-An was when she signed that first contract. So damn surprised and delighted to get publication they don't even read the *large* print. They just say 'Goody goody' and sign on the dotted line. The

24

kids without agents, and it's damn near as hard to get a good agent to handle your stuff as it is to get a publisher to buy it cold. Has this got anything to do with somebody's getting killed?"

"I don't know that it has. I guess it hasn't. However—Miss Lacey didn't have an agent, I gather. And an agent would have got her better terms."

"She never had had, she told me. And any decent agent sure as hell would. Hell, I know one man who gets seventeen and a half after ten. Damn near everybody gets a break after twenty-five hundred copies. And another after five thousand. A break up, I mean. To twelve and a half first time; maybe to fifteen second time. See what I mean?"

"I guess so," Shapiro said. And he thought he was wasting time.

"*And* half the movie money," Shepley said. There was bitterness in his voice. He finished his drink. "Which in her case came to one hell of a lot. And, you won't believe this, she didn't even get an advance on any of the books. Not one God-damn cent."

He banged the bell again. This time the waiter came almost at once. Shepley said, "You?" to Nathan Shapiro and Shapiro said, "No." Shepley said, "Old Crow and plain water," to the waiter, who said, "Yes, sir," and went away.

"The only thing those people didn't get," Shepley said, "was an option in perpetuity on the same terms. I don't know how they missed that one. It's been done. Karn's option expired with *Snake*. So I got her to promise to go to Phil Morton before she signed anything else."

"Karn? Morton?"

"Oscar Karn, Incorporated. Phil Morton—Phillips Morton, Incorporated—is an agent. Mine, as a matter of fact. He'd grab her. Maybe—maybe he already has. She said—when we made this lunch date—she had a lot to tell me. And he's one of the best. Get her a straight fifteen, at the least. Maybe do better. And no split on the movie money. That's drying up too, but there's still some around."

The waiter brought a glass with whisky in it and ice and a

25

small pitcher of water. Shepley said, "Thanks," and pushed a ten-dollar bill on the table. The waiter said, "Thank *you*, sir," and went away with the ten-dollar bill.

"She told you all about this in those conversations you had," Shapiro said. "About her contract, I mean."

"Yes," Shepley said, and all at once he smiled through his red beard. "What did you think writers talk about when they get together? The art of fiction?"

Shapiro said he wouldn't know.

Mackenowitz's studio was in West Twelfth Street, beyond Eighth Avenue toward the river. It was an easy enough walk on a pleasant early summer day. The wind was from the southwest, which probably meant that by tomorrow the air would thicken. But this was today, and one could still breathe the air. Tony walked northwest on West Fourth Street. Of course, Rachel might have finished the stint and put her clothes on and gone on to lunch or to the next job. On the other hand, it was conceivable that she hadn't gone to lunch yet and that he could take her. He'd have to have lunch anyway.

He turned left into West Twelfth, not hurrying—feeling good and thinking of Rachel Farmer. The building he lived in was near Eighth Avenue, and as he approached it he saw a Negro woman going heavily up the steps which led to the front door. Even from a little distance there was something vaguely familiar about her. She was opening the door to the vestibule when he came to the foot of the stairs. He still wasn't sure, but he said, "Mrs. Jenkinson?" and she turned and faced him.

"You're that cop," she said. "What you following me for, man?"

"I'm a cop," Tony Cook said. "I'm not following you."

She said, "So all right," and pulled the door open.

"It's where I live," Tony said. "It happens I was just passing by, but it's where I live. You weren't coming to see me? About Miss Jones or anything?"

"What would I be coming to see you about?" she said. "I told you and those other policemen all I know about Miss

26

Jones—the poor thing. I'm just going up to do the gentleman's place, like I've been doing once a week."

Tony lives on the second floor of the house in West Twelfth. A couple lives on the floor above. Tony said, "That would be Mr. Shepley?"

"It sure would, man. You got any objections?"

Her voice was tired. Probably, Tony thought, she was tired all over. She'd come down early by subway from Harlem; she had found a woman dead in a bathtub. Which didn't mean she didn't still have to clean for the others she cleaned for on Friday. And probably on Saturday too.

"Why would I have?" Tony said. "Go on up, Mrs. Jenkinson. And take it easy."

The last sentence sounded pretty ridiculous as he said it. It apparently sounded equally ridiculous to Mrs. Jenkinson.

"Take it easy, the man says," she said, with tired contempt in her voice. She went on into the vestibule. Tony saw her press a bell button and listened for the click of the released inner door lock. He didn't hear it. Mrs. Jenkinson reached into her handbag and got a key out and used it and went into the building. She'd have three steep flights of stairs to climb before she could get to work, Tony thought, and walked on west through the pleasant early summer day.

It was only a coincidence, Tony thought, as he waited for the lights to change at Eighth Avenue. And it wasn't much of one. Every Tuesday a woman came down from Harlem to do his own apartment, and she could give him only an hour before she had four more to do for in the neighborhood. A friend of his had given him the woman's name, and she was regular and cleaned well enough. And, of course, she had her key to the outer door and to his apartment.

The light changed, and he crossed Eighth Avenue and walked on west.

Of course, the way you usually got hold of cleaning women was through somebody who already had one with a little time to spare. It was just a coincidence that Mrs. Jenkinson, who had worked for Miss Jones in Gay Street, also worked for Mr. Shepley in West Twelfth—Mr. Shepley with the groomed red beard. Probably Mrs. Jenkinson worked for a dozen people in Greenwich Village. Any one of them could have told her that Shepley needed a cleaning woman. Or that Miss Jones did. Tony found that he was, in his mind, putting "Miss Jones" in quotation marks. Which was making an assumption. A lot of people are named Jones.

He came to a tall, narrow building near Hudson Street. It had the appearance of a loft building. He checked in the tiny, grimy lobby. Ivan Mackenowitz was on the fifth floor. He climbed stairs and when he came to the top of them knocked on a door. A man's voice, very gruff and loud, answered his knocking. The man said, "I don't want anything."

Tony pushed at the door and it opened. He looked into a large bright room with a skylight. Rachel was standing on what appeared to be a low platform. She wasn't wearing anything. A man who seemed to be much smaller than his voice was standing facing her, at an easel. When he turned to face Tony he said, "What the hell do you want?"

"It's all right, Ivan," Rachel Farmer said. "He's a friend of mine. Hi, Tony. What *do* you want?"

"We're working," Ivan Mackenowitz said. "Can't you see we're working, whoever you are?"

Anthony Cook said who he was and that he wanted a word with Miss Farmer.

Rachel came down off the platform and sat in a chair in front of canvases stacked against the wall.

"And put a robe on," Ivan Mackenowitz told her.

She said, "Oh, all right," in a tone of tolerance for the idiosyncrasies of others, and went across the room and picked a robe off another chair and put it on. She went back to the first chair and sat on it again. She said, "What about, Tony?"

"This woman you saw typing at that window," Tony said. "The one you told me about. She's dead, Rachel. We think somebody killed her."

Rachel Farmer said, "Oh. Oh, *no*, Tony." He saw her throat move as she swallowed. She said, "But she seemed to be working so hard. Bent down over the typewriter and working so hard."

28

"I know," Tony said. "It's a hell of a thing. Can you tell me what she looked like, Rachel? Would you have known her if you'd met her someplace?"

"No," Rachel said. "She was—I told you, Tony—she was just sort of a shadow. The light was on the typewriter. She was just —oh, just a shape with the light behind her."

"A young shape? Or an old shape?"

"Not old, I'd think. She—I think she had hair almost down to her shoulders. I don't know what color. I really don't, Tony."

"She was sitting there at the typewriter only in the evenings? And at night. After dinner. Every night, do you think?"

"I don't know. I didn't go past there every night. Mostly when I did, I think. When the window was open I would hear the typewriter going and look up and think—oh, how hard she was working."

"Do you remember when you first saw her?"

Rachel hesitated. She shook her head slightly. She said, "Perhaps a month ago? A little more or a little less. Yes, I'd think about a month ago. But it's no good, Tony. I can't tell you what she looked like. Or whether she was sitting there every night. Somebody killed her?"

"It was meant to look like suicide," Tony said, "but we don't think it was—that is, Nate and I don't think it was. She—well, she was in the bathtub with her wrists cut."

Rachel said, "Oh!" again and put her right hand up to her lips. She shook her head again, her hand still pressing against her lips. She took the hand down and said, "I'm sorry, Tony. She was—she was just a shadow in the light."

"There's nothing to be sorry about," Tony said. "We're—oh, as usual, just trying to put the pieces together. Are you about finished here? Because if you are—"

"She's not," Ivan Mackenowitz said, his voice gruffer than ever. "Won't be for an hour, Mr. Anthony Cook. An hour and a half if you keep on asking her damn-fool questions."

"He's like that, Tony," Rachel said. "Most of them are like that."

She slipped the robe off and went back to stand on the little platform. She stood, so far as Tony could tell, exactly as she had stood before.

"The head," Mackenowitz said. "Damn it, Miss Farmer, the *head*."

She moved her head a little. Tony said, "Tomorrow, then?" and, without moving her head, which was turned a little away from him, Rachel said, "Of course, Tony."

4

People kept coming into the lobby of the Hotel Algonquin and kept going out of it. Most of those who went out went through the entrance to the restaurant. Some went into the Rose Room, which was also a restaurant with an illuminated sign, "Cocktails." A few went out into Forty-fourth Street, but more came in from it. Laurence Shepley drank bourbon; Nathan Shapiro sipped from his glass of sherry. Sour it was, he thought; almost bitter sour. Why not call it that instead of calling it "dry"?

"When you took Miss Lacey home from dinner," Shapiro said, "did you ever take her to Gay Street, Mr. Shepley? Or did you ever call for her there? Visit her there?"

"I don't know where this Gay Street is," Shepley said. "She lives—lived, I guess—here at the Algonquin." He finished his drink and started to stand up. He said, "I'm going to have lunch. You want to come along?"

"No," Shapiro said. "And I'd appreciate it if you gave me a few more minutes before you have your lunch. There ought to be pictures of her coming along pretty soon. I'd like you to have a look at them."

"Taken after she was dead? This Miss Jones you think was Jo-An was dead?"

"Yes."

"I don't much want to look at pictures of dead people."

"Nobody does much, Mr. Shepley. Some of us have to. Meanwhile—you say she dressed well. You did say that, didn't you?"

"I guess I did. Yeah, she dressed well."

"There weren't any of her clothes in the Gay Street place," Shapiro said. "Oh, a white dress and things to go with it."

"I don't know," Shepley said. "I think she wore a white dress once or twice."

"If Miss Lacey and Miss Jones are—were—the same person, her clothes will be up in her room, probably," Shapiro said. "I'd like you to go up with me and have a look at them."

"Proving what? We know Jo-An lived here."

Proving, Nathan Shapiro thought, I want to see how you react to things. "Probably nothing," Shapiro said. "We may come across somebody downtown who saw Miss Jones wearing the same clothes. Going into her apartment. Gives us a tie-in, if you see what I mean."

"A pretty fuzzy one," Shepley said. "Look, am I under arrest or something?"

"Not at all. Go have your lunch if you want to. Or, cooperate with the police. Either way you want it."

"Without prejudice?"

"Well—no official prejudice, Mr. Shepley. I'd like your help is all."

"O.K. All right, O.K. Damn it all, man, I saw her in them. Her clothes, I mean. Now they—well, they'll just be hanging there, limp. Anyhow, they'll make a fuss about letting us in the room."

"Not too much of a fuss," Shapiro said. He stood up. Shepley, who had interrupted his own movement to stand, looked up at him.

"All right," Shepley said, in a low, slow voice, "I wasn't sleeping with Jo-An. Or planning to, come to that. But—well, she was a damn nice kid."

"Kid? According to the autopsy report, the dead woman was in her late twenties or early thirties."

"Jo-An was a kid all the same. A—a bright, expectant kid.

She was going to have lunch with me today. She liked it here. She—it was a change from Alabama for her. One hell of a change. She'd read about the Algonquin, I guess. About Frank Adams and Dorothy Parker and Woollcott and the rest. Long time ago, that was. Before my time. Before her time. All right, let's go look at her clothes."

He stood up. He walked to the hotel desk, leading Shapiro.

The desk clerk did make something of a fuss. The assistant manager, summoned from his office behind the desk, looked at Shapiro's badge and said it was irregular, wasn't it? but he guessed so and he'd have a bellman go up with them. Outside the door of Room Nine-twelve, the bellman said, "Something happened to the lady? On account of, I used to get cabs for her sometimes. And brought her gear up when she first arrived. She was a pleasant lady, talked sort of Southern. Something's happened to her?"

"We can't be sure yet," Shapiro said, and the bellman used a key and let them into Room Nine-twelve. It was a moderately large room with twin beds—with two easy chairs and a long chest which had a mirror over it and a glass top. There was a small, straight chair in front of the low chest. There were cosmetics in bottles and boxes on the top of the chest. Somebody had been living in this room. It wasn't like the apartment in Gay Street, in which it was hard to believe anybody had ever lived.

Shapiro opened the closet door and dresses and a light coat and a long negligee were on hangers in it. He said, "Have a look, will you, Mr. Shepley?" and Shepley went to the closet and began to slide dresses along on the rod, looking at each. Shapiro went into the bathroom. There were two toothbrushes in slots of the receptacle for the bathroom glass. In the medicine cabinet there was a tube of toothpaste and a hairbrush and a bottle of Maalox. There were no bottles containing sleeping pills.

Shapiro went back into the bedroom. Shepley was still looking at the clothes in the closet. He had taken two dresses out of it and laid them on one of the beds.

Shapiro put a handkerchief over his fingers and opened a

small drawer in the desk section of the chest. The drawer contained stationery marked "Hotel Algonquin." He looked in the drawer under the first one, still with the handkerchief shielding his fingers. He found a flat checkbook of a national bank in Mobile, Alabama. The checks in it were printed, "Jo-An Lacey."

She had filled in her slips carefully, in a small, clear hand. She had tallied them. Her balance in the Mobile bank was, to Nathan Shapiro, rather surprisingly large. Rose and Nathan Shapiro keep whatever spare cash they have, which is never a great deal, mostly in a savings bank.

Shepley came out of the closet and pointed to the two dresses he had spread out on the bed.

"Those two I'm pretty sure of," he said. "Pretty sure I've seen her wearing them, I mean."

Both the dresses were summer afternoon dresses. One of them was a print of yellow and black. The other was a long-sleeved white dress with a low V in the back.

"There's another one I'm not quite sure about," Shepley said. He brought a gray dress of what Shapiro thought was lightweight wool out of the closet. It was a dress with a dark gray top and a skirt slashed with deep red and the same dark gray. It was a little longer than the other two when Shepley laid it out on the bed beside them. Shapiro memorized the three dresses and said, "All right, Mr. Shepley. Sorry to have held up your lunch."

They went down together, with the bellman, to the street level. Tony Cook was at the hotel desk, talking to the room clerk. Shapiro went up to him and Cook said, "I've got the—oh, hello, Mr. Shepley."

Shepley had started toward the restaurant, but he turned back. He looked at Tony, at first blankly. Then he said, "Hi, neighbor." He looked from Tony Cook to Nathan Shapiro. "You two seem to know each other," he said. "Don't tell me you're a cop too, neighbor?"

"Cook," Tony said. "Yes, I'm a cop too. I've got some pictures, Lieutenant."

He took pictures out of a manila envelope. The top one

34

showed a young woman lying in a bathtub, with long hair floating on grimy water. Tony took out another picture, this one only of head and shoulders. It was a picture of the same young woman. Death was spread out on both pictures.

"Have a look at this, will you, Mr. Shepley?" Shapiro said and held out the picture which showed only head and shoulders.

Laurence Shepley looked at the photograph. He said, "Jesus," in a slow voice—a voice with shock in it. Then he said, "Do they always look like that, Lieutenant?"

"Pretty much," Shapiro said. "Is it Miss Lacey?"

"Yes," Shepley said. "It's Jo-An. And—this Miss Jones?"

It was Tony Cook who said "Yes" to that. Shapiro looked at the man with the red beard for a moment. Then he said, "You can go have your lunch now, Mr. Shepley."

Shepley didn't say anything. He walked away, but not toward the restaurant entrance. He walked along by the partition toward the door and Forty-fourth Street.

"I want Room Nine-twelve kept locked until some men get here," Shapiro told the desk clerk. "Nobody goes into it. You understand that, Mr. Arthur?"

"I'll get the man—"

"Just keep the room locked up," Shapiro said. "Don't let anybody into it. That's a police order."

The desk clerk said, "Yes, Lieutenant."

Shapiro said, "Come on, Tony," and then, "No. Wait a minute."

He went to a row of telephone booths and pulled a Manhattan directory out of the rack. Phillips Morton, Inc., had an office at 529 Fifth Avenue, which would be convenient. Shapiro went into one of the booths and dialed the number he wanted. Precinct would be notified; the lab squad and the fingerprint men would go over Room 912 at the Hotel Algonquin.

Tony Cook and Nathan Shapiro walked east on Forty-fourth Street. They were two tall men, one in slacks and sports jacket, the other in a tired gray suit. Although it was warming

35

up, they both kept their jackets buttoned to cover the guns under them.

"Shepley is a writer," Shapiro said. "Says he is, at any rate. And a friend of Miss Lacey's, who also was a writer. A much better-known one, Shepley says. A famous one, he says. Not a particularly close friend of Miss Lacey's, Shepley says he wasn't. Bought her a few drinks. A dinner or two. Says he's never been in Gay Street."

"He lives in the Village," Cook said. "Same building I live in. An easy walk from it to Gay Street. And, he was at the bar at Charles Restaurant last night while Rachel and I were there. Waiting for somebody to join him, it could have been."

"He was waiting back there," Shapiro said, "at the hotel. For Miss Lacey to join him for lunch. He seems to bob up a bit, doesn't he, Tony?"

Tony Cook agreed that Shepley seemed to bob up quite a bit.

"And," he said, "the woman who worked for Miss Lacey when she was Miss Jones in Gay Street also works for Shepley. Cleans his apartment once a week. This Mrs. Jenkinson. Probably just a coincidence. Like your running into Shepley at the Algonquin. Where Miss Lacey was staying."

"Where she was living," Shapiro said. "The Gay Street place and the false name—just a hideaway or a front or something. Yes, it's still here."

It was the unmarked police car. Tony held his hand out for the key.

"No," Shapiro said. "We won't need it just yet."

He told Cook where they were going and why they wouldn't need a car to get there. They waited for lights to cross Fifth Avenue.

"Did you find Miss Farmer?" Shapiro asked.

Cook told about finding Rachel, and that Rachel had never got a good look at the woman at the typewriter. "Which doesn't matter now, of course," he said. "We know what she looked like." He said that it was when he was walking toward the studio where she was posing that he had seen Mrs. Jenkinson climbing the steps to the house he lived in.

36

"The pix went downtown?" Shapiro said, as the lights changed and they crossed Fifth Avenue. Cook said that the pictures had gone downtown for the precinct men to show around. They found 529 Fifth Avenue, which was a tall building. "Morton, Phillips, Authors' Representative" had office 1012. They went up to the tenth floor and along a corridor. PHILLIPS MORTON, INC., AUTHORS' REPRESENTATIVE was on the ground glass of a door. They opened the door into a small office with a young woman sitting at a typewriter. She was filing her nails.

"We'd like to see Mr. Morton," Shapiro told her.

"I'm afraid he's gone to lunch," the girl said, and kept on filing her nails. Then she looked up at Nathan Shapiro. She looked, Shapiro thought, with skepticism. Probably, Nathan thought, because he didn't look like an author. I look, Shapiro thought, like a slightly seedy character approaching middle age. She looked at Tony Cook with, Shapiro realized, considerably more animation. "I'm sorry he's out," she told Tony Cook. "He probably won't be back until around three. If he comes back at all, that is."

But then the door from the corridor opened and a man of middle height and medium roundness came in. He had a towel on his right hand. The girl said, "Oh, Mr. Morton, I thought you'd gone. These gentlemen—"

"Washing my hands," Phillips Morton said. He had a brisk voice. He was, Nathan Shapiro thought, probably in his middle thirties. "Afraid I've got to be getting along, though. You gentlemen wanted to see me? Haven't got much time. Going to lunch with an editor. So?"

Shapiro said who he was and who Tony Cook was. Morton said, "Why me? I haven't run over anybody or anything."

"About Miss Lacey," Shapiro said. "Miss Jo-An Lacey. A client of yours, we've been told."

"Just moved into my stable," Morton said. "Coming in Monday to sign a contract."

"No," Shapiro said, "I'm afraid she isn't, Mr. Morton. I'm afraid she's dead."

Morton's round, reddened face seemed to freeze. He said,

37

"God damn it to hell." He shook his head. He said, "God damn it to *hell*." Then he said, "Wouldn't you *know?*" He said, "Come on in," and led the way to a door across the little room. He put his hand on the doorknob and turned back. He said, "Get the Algonquin, will you, honey? Have them page Bracken. Have them tell him I'm held up and'll be there as soon as I can and to start his drinking."

The girl said, "Yes, Mr. Morton."

Morton said, "Come on," and opened the door and went through it. Shapiro and Cook went after him into a somewhat larger room with a desk backed to a window. Morton went to the chair behind the desk and motioned toward two other chairs. He said to Shapiro, "You're a police lieutenant?"

"Yes. Homicide."

"Don't tell me Miss Lacey's been killed?"

"I just did," Shapiro said. "And we want to know what you knew about her. And about a man named Laurence Shepley."

"Damn little about her," Morton said. "Except what everybody knows. Big hit with *Snake Country*. Big movie sale. And boy, did she get gypped. Shep—hell, I've known Shep for years. Handled him for years. Nothing flashy. Steady producer. Was until the magazines started to fold, anyway. What do you want to know?"

"Whatever you can tell us. You said—what was it?—that she'd just moved into your stable."

"Got her on my list," Morton said. "If you'd rather have it that way. And damn glad to have her there." He paused and shook his head. He said, "*Jesus!*" Then he said, "Old Shep gave her my name. Thoughtful of him. Realized, I guess from something she told him, she needed somebody." He looked intently at Shapiro. "A hell of a writer," he said. "But, without somebody like me—an agent who knows his way around—a sheep for the shearing."

"Mr. Shepley suggested she come to you," Shapiro said. "She did. When was that, Mr. Morton?"

It had been, Morton told them, about two weeks ago. He riffled back in a desk calendar and said, "Monday, June twelfth." She had called him up and said that Shepley had suggested she get in touch with him. "As soon as she told me her name, I said to come right around. Because—well, she's the kind of writer agents dream about. You're sure she's dead?"

Shapiro said he was afraid so. He said, "Go ahead, Mr. Morton."

Jo-An Lacey had come right around. She had brought part of a manuscript. "Four chapters. Carbon, but partly corrected." She had also brought a copy of her old contract with a publisher. She said she had been told she could do better.

"I looked over her contract and said, 'My God, lady!' Something like that, anyway."

She had left the four chapters of the manuscript with him. She had also left her contract.

"You and she signed some sort of an agreement? Appointing you as her representative?"

"Not the way it's done," Morton said. "Not by me, anyway. Oral agreement. Sure, in the contract there's an agency clause. The book contract, I mean. The one she was going to sign this afternoon. Damn good contract. Straight fifteen to twenty thousand. Seventeen and a half from there on. Sixty per cent of the paperback and the rest of the subsidiaries. No grab at the movie rights or first serial or foreign rights. Materson was tickled pink to get her. Ten thousand advance and I could have got a lot more, but she didn't want a lot more."

"You took this part of her book to—to whom, Mr. Morton?"

"Materson and Brothers. They're old line—solid old line. One of the best in the business. And they're not about to merge with anybody, far's I know."

He had taken the first four chapters of a book which had, as a working title, "Lonely Waters." He had read them that same night and had submitted them to Materson the next day. They had read the material in a week. "Which must be pretty close to a record." They had accepted the novel. "Without even an outline of the rest of it. That's how sure they were." Materson & Brothers had accepted what he had demanded in the contract. "Not a whimper out of them. That's how anxious they were to get her." He had got the contract for her signature on Wednesday the twenty-first and called her. She had been going to come in next Monday and sign it. God damn it to hell. "If only I'd made her come right away."

"She expected to finish the manuscript when, Mr. Morton?"

"She'd brought it up with her. Lived down in Alabama somewhere. Had been revising it up here—for several weeks, I gathered. Thought she could turn it in by Monday; sign the contract when she brought the rest of the book."

"Have you any idea where the complete manuscript is, Mr. Morton?"

"In her room at the hotel, I suppose. She was staying at the Algonquin. Sort of—oh, a sanctuary, you'd almost call it—for a lot of writing kids. Like Sardi's is for the theater people, if you know what I mean."

Nathan Shapiro didn't. He nodded his head anyway. He said, "Did she say anything to you about Gay Street, Mr. Morton?"

Morton repeated "Gay Street?" and shook his head.

"She had an apartment there," Shapiro said. "She used the name Jones. That's where she died. In the Gay Street apartment. She apparently had been working there. But there wasn't any manuscript there. Nor any sign of the typewriter she'd been using."

Phillips Morton said he didn't get it.

"Neither do we, so far," Shapiro said.

"Sometimes," Morton said, "writers do rent places to work in. Away from where they're living. Offices, in a way. So they won't get interrupted. You say she called herself Jones?"

"A. Jones. No first name. Unlisted telephone."

"That's it," Morton said. "She was—oh, sort of hiding out so she could get the work done."

"Probably. What happens now? About the book she was just finishing? About the contract she was going to sign?"

"I'm damned if I know," Morton said. "When you find the manuscript, what'll be done with it?"

"Property clerk to start with," Shapiro said. "Then to her estate. I don't suppose she said anything about that? Or about a will she might have made?"

"Hell," Morton said, "she was about thirty, Lieutenant. People don't make wills when they're about thirty."

"The contract? What about it?"

"It's not signed. So it's waste paper."

"Her previous contract? The one you say she was gypped on?"

"Two-book option," Morton said. "It ran out with her last one. With the big-hit one—*Snake Country*."

"And you had only this oral agreement appointing you as her agent for—what was the name of the book?"

"'Lonely Waters,' she called it. Not the hottest title in the world, to my way of thinking. Materson probably would have talked her into changing it. Water under the bridge now, I guess. Oh, about our agreement. It's water under the bridge too. So, I'm left with ten per cent of nothing."

"Ten per cent?"

"The agent's fee. You don't know much about this business, do you, Lieutenant?"

Shapiro had been thinking the same thing. Life had been simpler years ago when he was a patrolman on a Brooklyn beat. He said he didn't know much about the business of writing and publishing books.

"All right," Morton said, and he was patient. "If she'd lived to sign this contract, they'd have sent me the advance of ten thousand. Made out to Phillips Morton, Incorporated, as agent. I'd have banked the money and sent her a check for nine thousand. Same with the royalties when they started coming in. Ten per cent cut down the line. For knowing markets, knowing about contracts. Doing the paper work. Seeing your people don't get gypped, the way Karn—"

He stopped speaking abruptly. He said, "I shouldn't say that. That would be slander, wouldn't it? Highly respectable company, Oscar Karn, Incorporated. Let's just say they drive a shrewd bargain, huh? Not that they're in the business of fleecing the innocent. Huh?"

"Oscar Karn, Incorporated?"

"Published her first three books. Let's just say I've got her— I had got her—a better contract from Materson and Brothers.

And old Oscar'll be—would have been—fit to be tied. They used to bring out a lot of hits. Haven't had one for the last—oh, three years. Last they had was Miss Lacey's, as a matter of fact. Been counting on her new one to—well, get them going again. All right, that's just gossip. So's the report the Jefferson Press is going to take Karn over. They'll call it a merger. Sure. But it's a takeover."

"You've lost me," Shapiro said. "As you've gathered, Mr. Morton, I'm easy to lose in things like this."

"Oscar Karn, Incorporated, is in trouble," Morton said. "Jefferson Press, which isn't—almost as well fixed as Materson, actually—is buying it out, according to what's going around in the trade. If old Oscar'd got 'Lonely Waters' it would have been, could be, the shot in the arm he needed. At the least, it would have upped Jefferson's price one hell of a lot. Clear enough?"

"Quite clear. And as things stand now, the Karn company has no claim on Miss Lacey's new book. Assuming the manuscript turns up?"

"I told you that. Their option ran out with *Snake Country*. It'll be a whole new deal. With me dealt out, probably. Unless —well, unless her estate decides to go along with the Materson contract. As it will if it's in its right mind. Only, where is its mind?"

"She didn't tell you anything about her family? If she had a family?"

"Why should she? Wait a minute—just wait a minute."

Shapiro waited.

"When the snake-country novel turned out to be the hit it was," Morton said, "there was quite a bit written about Jo-An Lacey. Karn's publicity department got busy, of course. There was a long interview with her—sort of a profile, actually—in the *Times*. I read it. Skimmed it, anyway. Never expected to get her in my stable." He paused. He shook his head. He said, "God damn it to hell!" He said, "Seems to me there was something in it about her having a brother. Wait a minute."

Shapiro waited. "It's beginning to come back a little," Morton said. He was speaking slowly now. "Old family estate somewhere outside Mobile, Alabama. Wait a minute. Not an estate. A 'plantation.' The Lacey Plantation. That was it. Been in the Lacey family since God knows when. Cotton?"

He seemed to expect an answer. Shapiro said he didn't know.

"Anyway, she lived there with her brother, and the implication in this *Times* piece was that they were strapped until she started writing. Last of the Laceys, that sort of thing. Can't remember the brother's name."

He paused again and shook his head.

"Beauregard?" Tony Cook suggested.

Morton did not rise to it. He merely said it didn't sound quite right.

"Aristocrats of the Old South," Morton said. "That sort of thing. Big rambling house. Probably used to be called the Lacey Mansion or something. Can't think why—wait a minute. In this interview they asked her what she planned to do now, with a lot of money coming in. And she said she'd go on living at home, of course, and use some of the money to fix the place up. And, yes, she'd go on writing. About the places and the people she knew about. *Snake Country* was Southern as all hell. I don't mean molasses. It was a damn good book. But Southern as all hell."

"This new book of hers is too?"

"From what I read of it, yes. You get a good thing going, you keep it going. Also, what else would she know to write about? Immured way down there in—well, in snake country, I suppose. Not that I know anything about southern Alabama."

"If her new manuscript doesn't turn up at the hotel," Shapiro said, "have you any idea where it might be, Mr. Morton?"

Morton said he didn't.

"She wouldn't have sent it in to this Oscar Karn company?"

"No reason she should have I can think of. Unless she sent it in before she saw me, and she didn't say anything about that. Only that she'd turn the whole manuscript over to me as soon as she'd finished with it. Why would she send it to Karn? Karn had no claim on it."

43

"She might have thought he had," Shapiro said. "It would be bulky, this manuscript?"

"Four or five hundred pages, she thought," Morton said. "Twice that with carbon. Three times that if she made two carbons. Yes, I'd call it bulky, Lieutenant."

In his mind, Nathan Shapiro went over the room Jo-An Lacey had had at the Algonquin. He hadn't really searched it; that was being done now, or would soon be being done. But four hundred pages of typescript—perhaps eight hundred or even twelve hundred—would make quite a bundle. Too big to fit into any of the drawers of the low chest, as he remembered it.

"Oscar Karn, Incorporated," he said. "Have you any idea offhand where their offices are, Mr. Morton?"

"Sure. I've sent enough manuscripts to them. Two floors up. Here in this building."

"Can you tell me anything more about Mr. Shepley, Mr. Morton?"

"What more? He's a good guy. He sells enough to live on and it's pretty good stuff. He used to sell quite a few short stories to the slicks, when they were buying fiction. Damn good, some of them were. Been doing articles last few years. What they want, what of them are left. And aren't all staff-written. A hell of a good guy, old Shep is. And—all right, not much more than getting by. Being a good guy doesn't help a free lance these days. Oh, yes, he's got a red beard. On him it looks good."

Morton passed a hand absently over his own clean-shaven face. He took the opportunity to look at the watch on his wrist. He said, his voice again abrupt, "Bracken will be under the table if I don't get there pretty soon."

"Go along, Mr. Morton," Shapiro said. "We'll be back if there's anything else we think you can help us with."

5

They walked down the corridor toward the banks of elevators. Both Shapiro and Tony Cook were taller than Phillips Morton, but he walked faster. He bustled ahead of them. He had already pressed a down button when they caught up with him. A car stopped for him and he bounced into it. The door of the car started to close but he put a hand on it, pressing against the pneumatic edging.

"Let it go, Mr. Morton," Shapiro said. "Before your friend is under the table."

Morton let the door close. Cook looked at Shapiro and raised his eyebrows.

"Suppose," Shapiro said, "you see what you can dig up about this Miss Lacey. And find out what they're doing downtown. And what they've found at the hotel, aside from the fingerprints which will tell us that Miss Jones was Miss Lacey. And, I suppose, see what the Mobile police can tell you. O.K.?"

Tony said, "Sir," in a tone which required a salute to go with it. They both laughed a little at that. Tony said, "And you, Lieutenant?"

"I'm a little curious about this Mr. Karn," Shapiro said. "The man who writes such bad contracts. And is, if Morton knows what he's talking about, about to be gobbled up."

"I don't see—" Tony said, and let it hang while he pressed a down button.

"Neither do I," Nathan Shapiro said, and pressed an up button. "I'm way out of my depth on the whole thing." He sighed. He shook a discouraged head.

Tony Cook didn't believe a word of it. He had heard it too often. A down car stopped and he got into it. Shapiro had to wait a while for an up car.

The twelfth-floor directory listed offices 1210–1218 for "Oscar Karn, Inc., Publishers." Room 1210 had the firm's name on it and the word "Entrance." The room was long and wide enough for a line of leather-covered sofas along one wall. The sofas were dented; it was evident that many people had sat on them. Two of the leather seats had splits in them.

At the far end of the room a middle-aged woman with gray hair was sitting behind a desk marked "Information." She had a telephone propped between shoulder and left ear and was talking into it. She said, "I'm sure you will hear any day now, Mr. Ferguson," and put the telephone back in its stand and said, "Can I help you?" to Nathan Shapiro. Shapiro said he'd like to see Mr. Karn and that no, he didn't have an appointment and told the gray-haired woman who she should say was calling. She said, "*Lieutenant* Shapiro?" He said, "A police lieutenant," and was told to wait a minute.

She lifted the telephone from its stand and pressed one of several buttons in its base. She waited a few seconds. She said, "There's a police lieutenant wants to see Mr. Karn, Maggie." She listened. She said, "No, he doesn't say what it's about. Hold on." She looked at Shapiro, who said, "About Miss Lacey. Miss Jo-An Lacey." She repeated the information to Maggie. Then she said, "Oh. I'll tell him," and put the telephone back. "I'm sorry," she said, "Mr. Karn seems to have gone for the weekend. His secretary says Monday perhaps?"

"I'd like to see him today," Shapiro said. "Would his secretary know where I might be able to find him?"

"Well, he has a place up in the country. He goes there most weekends in the summer."

"Where in the country?"

"Oh, I'm afraid I can't tell you that. Mr. Karn doesn't like to be disturbed on his weekends."

"Neither do I," Shapiro said. "Where, miss?"

She had pale blue eyes, which protruded a little. She looked up at Shapiro and her eyes seemed to protrude farther.

"It's police business," Shapiro said. "I'm afraid I'll have to ask you to tell me."

"It's against the—"

"I know," Shapiro said. "Against the rules. So is withholding information from the police. Where?"

"Outside Mount Kisco," she said. "Anybody can tell you where the Karn place is, I guess. Anybody around there. Only he'll probably be playing golf."

Shapiro sighed. He said, "Thank you, Miss—" and looked at the plaque on her desk. He said, "O'Ryan."

"Mrs. O'Ryan," the gray-haired woman said. "My husband was Terence O'Ryan. The writer."

Shapiro said, "Oh," and tried to make the sound one of enlightenment, as if he had heard of a writer named Terence O'Ryan. He said, "Thank you," again and, "Mrs. O'Ryan," and went out of the office. While the elevator dropped him, with uncomfortable precipitation, to the ground level, Shapiro hoped that Tony Cook hadn't taken the car. It's like me to have forgotten to tell him not to, Shapiro thought, and went across Fifth Avenue with the lights.

Tony Cook hadn't taken the car. I should have known he wouldn't, Shapiro thought, and unlocked the car and got into it. He drove to the corner and down Fifth a block and, slowly, through Forty-third Street toward the West Side Highway.

Tony Cook knew a man who worked in the morgue of the New York *Times*. It is helpful for a policeman to know people in a good many places. The envelope marked "Lacey, Jo-An" was not especially thick. The interview-profile Morton had spoken of had appeared on the second page of *The New York Times Book Review* and had jumped to Page 51.

Jo-An Lacey, whose recent novel, "Snake Country," has been on the best seller list for fourteen weeks, is a member of a family distinguished in the history of Alabama and of the South. A great-grandfather, General John Henry Lacey, was a distinguished cavalry officer during what Miss Lacey prefers to call "the war between the States." Her grandfather, John Willingham Lacey, was twice governor of Alabama in the late nineteenth century. The Lacey Mansion, in which Jo-An Lacey still lives, has been occupied by members of her family since the middle eighteenth century.

"And it's falling down on our heads," Miss Lacey says. "Now my book seems to be a success, I'm trying to prop it up again. That is, my brother and I are."

Her brother is John Henry Lacey III. He operates a real estate business from one of the many outbuildings on the Lacey plantation.

Miss Lacey is a slight, attractive woman, who looks younger than the thirty years she admits to. Her brown hair drifts down to her shoulders. Her speech is the speech of the deep South. There is constant animation and a kind of expectancy in her face as she talks of her work. "I just write about people I grew up among," she says. "The white people and the nigras. I suppose I shouldn't call them that nowadays. They want to be called 'blacks' now. But when I was little, we called them 'darkies' and I don't think they minded. They should have minded more, I think now. That is one of the things I've tried to make clear—make come alive—in 'Snake Country.' I'm not sure how well I've done it; how well I've got the feel of it."

Listening to Jo-An Lacey as she questions "how well she has done it," one is left feeling that there is no false modesty in her mind—that the praise of the critics and the wide—

The carry-over was clipped to the first sheet of newsprint. Tony read on in it.

"—and mounting public response to a novel which—"

Tony read further on. There was a good deal of it. There were other clippings in the envelope. Miss Jo-An Lacey had appeared on the "Today" show. She had been the guest of honor at a cocktail party given at the Hotel Pierre by P.E.N.; Leonard Lyons had attended a cocktail party given for her by her publishers, Oscar Karn, Inc. (he had been encountered by many celebrities at the party).

48

And it was, from the date on the paper, all a little more than three years ago. And it was thirty-six hours, give or take a few, since the animation and expectancy had bled out of Jo-An's face in a bathtub in a bare apartment in Gay Street.

Tony went down to Twenty-third Street by subway and walked along to Homicide South. He hoped Nate would remember that the police car was parked in Forty-fourth.

There were reports in the In basket on his desk. One was an addendum to the pathologist's report from the Bellevue morgue. Jo-An Lacey had become a number for the records. The barbiturate found in her body was Nembutal. She had not been a virgin. She had not had intercourse within forty-eight hours of her death. She had never borne a child. No organic impairment had been discovered. The amount of Nembutal taken would not, probably, have been in itself sufficient to have caused death.

Room 912 at the Hotel Algonquin was still, slowly and thoroughly, being taken apart. Fingerprints found in the room matched those found in the Gay Street apartment and those taken from the body.

Tony Cook looked up the telephone number of the Hotel Algonquin and dialed it and asked for Room 912 and got, "Yeah?" He identified himself. Yes, they were about finished. No, they had not found four or five hundred pages of typescript copy. They had found a checkbook and clothing which would be turned over to the property clerk. They had not found a book with telephone numbers listed in it. But they had found the stub of a telephone bill showing charges listed to "A. Jones." One of them was for a long-distance call made a week before. Judging by the charge, it had been a rather lengthy call. "Wait a minute." The call had lasted five minutes—a little over five minutes. It had been to Mobile, Alabama, and the number called had been—

Tony noted down the area code and the number. He said, "Thanks," to the man still in Room 912 and dialed the number he had been given. There were clicks and scratches and the murmur of mixed voices. Then there was the signal of a number being rung. It rang nine times unanswered before Tony gave it up.

The other tenants in the house on Gay Street had not heard anything out of the way going on in the apartment on the second floor. Yes, the couple on the third floor had heard a typewriter clattering below them for weeks. Not, so far as they could remember, the evening before. Perhaps not the evening before that. They had other things to do than listen to somebody else's typewriter. Nobody remembered hearing voices in the second-floor apartment or people moving around in it. "This is an old building. They built them solid when they built them then. Some of these new places—"

People had looked at prints of the head-and-shoulders view of the young woman who had called herself "A. Jones." People were still looking at the pictures, shown them by detectives from Charles Street and by uniformed men from the precinct. Policemen would be showing the pictures for many hours. So far they were getting shaken heads; they were getting "Maybes" and "Seems to me likes." They were getting nothing that helped—not in grocery stores or restaurants or in pharmacies; not in bars or boutiques or from hairdressers. "Seen this young lady around? Been a customer of yours?" They got shaken heads; they got, "Can't say that I have." They were working out with Gay Street as a center.

They had found the real estate agent who handled the apartment Jo-An Lacey had died in. There had been a young lady alone at a desk in the real estate office. She did not remember ever having seen the young woman of the photograph. "Of course, there are half a dozen of us here. It must have been one of the others who showed the apartment." Of course there were records. The apartment—let's see now. It was a furnished apartment and had been rented a month before to an A. Jones. No, there was no lease; the apartment had been rented on a monthly basis. At a hundred and seventy-five a month. Two months' rent had been paid in advance. "Here's a funny thing. This A. Jones person seems to have paid in cash. Sort of thing that doesn't happen much any more. Some of them try to pay with credit cards."

Captain William Weigand, commanding, came along the corridor from his office into the squad room. He stopped at Cook's desk and Cook stood up.

"Shapiro's got you with him on this Gay Street job, right?" Weigand said.

Tony said, "Yes, sir. We've found out who she was anyway, Captain. A writer named Lacey. Nate—I mean the lieutenant's gone to see her publisher."

"He called in," Weigand said. "He's on his way up to Mount Kisco to see this publisher. Who seems to be off on a weekend. Put a report through when you get around to it, Tony."

"Yes, sir."

"And how's Miss Farmer?"

"She—she's fine, sir."

"Oh," Weigand said, "things get around, Tony."

Tony Cook said it seemed like they did. He said, "Lieutenant Shapiro wants me to get in touch with the Mobile police about Miss Lacey. That O.K., Captain?"

"Of course," Weigand said. "It's your baby. Yours and Nate's."

He went out of the squad room and along the corridor outside and down the stairs. Through channels, Tony put in a call for somebody—anybody responsible—in the detective division of the Mobile Police Department. He waited five minutes and his telephone rang. He got, "Lieutenant Buncombe, go ahead," in a Southern male voice and then, "Yes, suh. Can I help you? This is Buncombe." There was a momentary pause. "B-u-n-c-o-m-b-e, that is."

"Detective Cook, New York Police, sir. We're after information about a Miss Lacey. Jo-An Lacey. Lives in Mobile. That is, she did live in Mobile."

"Not in the city," Buncombe said. "The Lacey Plantation's where she lives, Mr. Cook. Where they've all lived since before the war. Sure, everybody round hereabouts knows the Lacey family. Not that I mean knows, come to that. Specially since that book of hers. Think she went a bit far, some of us do."

All Buncombe's words sounded to Tony's New York ears as

51

if they were, obscurely, other words. He found he was translating as he went along.

"What you want to know about Miss Lacey?"

"I'm afraid," Tony said, "we want to know who killed her, sir."

"*Killed* her? Killed Jo-An *Lacey*? That's what you're saying, mister? Up there in New *York*?"

It was obvious that the location made a bad matter much worse to Lieutenant Buncombe. Laceys didn't go north to get killed.

"In an apartment in Greenwich Village."

"In *Green-witch* Village!"

As if "New York" had not been bad enough.

"She was using the name Jones," Tony Cook said. "But I'm afraid there's no doubt the deceased was Miss Lacey."

Lieutenant Buncombe repeated the name *"Jones"* in a tone of complete consternation. Bad matters could get no worse.

"This—er—plantation of the Laceys'? Far out of town, sir?"

"Outside the city limits a few miles. Tumbled down some, but she's—I mean her brother's—been putting it back together, sort of. Guess she must have made some money out of these books of hers. Place had been running down for years, from what I hear. People down here didn't think much of those books of hers. Felt she was running her own place down, sort of. Didn't read them myself."

"She and her brother lived on the plantation alone, sir?"

"Maybe a darky or two to help out. And men working on the house the last few years."

"There are other Laceys around there? Relatives?"

"Funny thing," Buncombe said, "mostly people have a lot of relatives. Cousins and the like. Can't seem to think of any for them, somehow. Their parents got killed years ago. Went up in an airplane and it ran into a mountain. Just Jo-An and that brother of hers. John Henry Three, he's called. Supposed to run some kind of real estate business, from what I hear. Thing is, mister, they're not in our territory. Sheriff's the man you want, come down to it."

"We'll get on to it, sir. Happen to know whether they've got a telephone? The Laceys, I mean."

"Be in—hold it a minute and I'll look."

Cook held it for rather more than a minute.

"Yep. John Henry Lacey Three. Want the number?"

Cook did. He got it. It was the number he had supposed it would be—the number which had not answered to its ringing. He thanked Lieutenant Buncombe, who said, "Any time, mister," and then, "Suah is too bad about Jo-An."

Tony Cook put the receiver back. Almost at once it rang at him. He said, "Cook," into it.

"Hi, Tony. Pieronelli. Maybe we're onto something. Know that restaurant over on Bank Street? Call it 'André's,' but it's Italian all the same."

"Yes," Tony said. "I know it, Charley. Damned good lasagna."

"That's the place. Well, seems our Miss Jones went in there now and then. At least, the headwaiter's pretty sure. Says it's a lousy picture—makes her look dead, he says—but he's pretty sure. I told him it wasn't the picture made her look dead. He thinks she came in for dinner three-four times last month or so. Remembers because the first time she didn't tip much and then, way he puts it, got wised up and tipped too much, if anything."

"She was from the deep South," Tony said. "Name of Lacey. Wrote novels. She went into the place alone?"

"Way he remembers it, she was alone the first couple of times. After that a man was with her."

"The man, Charley?"

"This headwaiter—his name's Lorenzo, not André—thinks the man with her had a beard. Not that that means much nowadays. That's all he remembers about him. Just that he maybe had a beard."

"Color of same?"

"He doesn't remember that, Tony. Just a beard."

"The last time they were in together?"

"Two-three nights ago, he thinks."

"He wouldn't be able to identify the man, I suppose?"

"Nope. Just a beard. No special color beard."

It wasn't much. As Charles Pieronelli had pointed out, there were a lot of beards around. By no means all of them were red.

Tony dialed the Alabama number. This time there was an answer after four rings. The answer was, "Lace resdunce." The second time Tony got it, he asked for Mr. Lacey.

"Ain't heah, suh. Ain't been heah fo bout a week maybe."

"Who's this?"

"I'se Henry, suh. Works for Mistuh Lacey and the lady."

"Do you know where Mr. Lacey has gone, Henry?"

"Seems like he went up no-th, suh. Way it seems to me, suh. Called somebody and asked about when trains went, seems like."

"If he comes back," Tony said, "ask him to call this number, will you?" and gave him the telephone number of Homicide, Manhattan South. "And ask for Detective Anthony Cook."

"Wha's that, suh?"

"New York City. A Police Department number. Will you tell him?"

"Yassuh. I'll suah do that, suh."

The four-to-midnight shift was beginning to drift in. Tony looked at his watch. The four-to-midnight was getting in on time.

Tony lighted a cigarette. Nate ought to be showing up pretty soon, or calling in. I ought to write a report. But about what that means a damn? Better wait until Shapiro shows.

He waited half an hour and Shapiro did not show. He went along home.

6

The man behind the counter served Nathan Shapiro a hamburger and two cups of surprisingly good coffee, and sure he knew the Karn place, and that if you went up One-seventeen for maybe a mile or so and turned right on Green Lane and then, after maybe about another mile, turned left, you couldn't miss it.

The last words thudded dully into Nathan Shapiro's mind. He has heard them often. People, in that one respect, are likely to underestimate me, he thought. I can miss anything.

He went to the car. He found Route 117 with little difficulty, although traffic considerably delayed him. He even found Green Lane. What he thought was the turnoff to the left was somebody's driveway, and a large German shepherd barked at him with what appeared to be fury. The next left turn wasn't anybody's driveway. And, after about a quarter of a mile, there was a driveway with a sign saying "The Karns" beside it. Shapiro turned up this driveway, which was of impeccably raked gravel. The drive led to a wide white house, with white pillars supporting a balcony. Shapiro parked the police car in the big, empty turnaround. He parked it facing out.

The man who answered the door wore a white jacket. Broad, heavy shoulders strained the jacket. He said, "Yes?" in the tone one uses to a man selling encyclopedias or the religion of Jehovah's Witnesses. Shapiro said he would like to see Mr. Karn.

"Mr. Karn is playing golf," the man in the white jacket said. "Always does Friday afternoon. He and Mrs. Karn both." He looked at Shapiro thoughtfully. He made up his mind. He added, "Sir."

"Have you any idea when he'll be back?"

The man in the white jacket looked at the watch on his wrist. Shapiro looked at his own watch. It was a little after four o'clock. No wonder he had needed the hamburger.

"Hard to tell, sir. Sometimes he plays late. But there're people coming in for drinks, and he'll probably—" He stopped, looking beyond Nathan Shapiro, and Shapiro heard the crunch of tires on the gravel. The car was a black Cadillac.

"Here he is now," the man in the white jacket said and went past Shapiro and down to the Cadillac. A rather short and moderately broad man got out from behind the wheel. He wore a neatly trimmed gray beard. The white jacket went to the other side of the car and opened the door, and a woman in shorts, who was several inches taller than the man, got out.

Shapiro went down toward the Cadillac. The woman came around the car. She said, "You're the TV man, I hope?"

"No," Shapiro said. "I'm a—"

"Damn," the woman said. "You just can't count on them."

She went across the gravel toward the house, golf shoes crunching.

The gray-bearded man, who was, Shapiro guessed, somewhere in his middle sixties, held out keys toward the man in the white jacket without looking at him.

He said, "Trouble with the color. Everything comes out pinkish. You wanted to see me?"

"If you're Mr. Oscar Karn, yes," Shapiro said.

"I'm Karn," the man said. He had a low, rather grating, voice.

"I'm a police lieutenant," Shapiro said. He added his name to it. He said, "From the city, Mr. Karn."

Karn merely raised bushy gray eyebrows.

"About Miss Jo-An Lacey," Shapiro said. "One of your writers, we understand."

56

"Yes. What about her?"

"Whatever you can tell us," Shapiro said. "You see, Mr. Karn, Miss Lacey's dead."

Karn looked at him. His eyes went blank and the face under the neat beard seemed to sag. After some seconds he said, "Dead?"

"Yes," Shapiro said. "I'm sorry to say she is, Mr. Karn. And, we think, murdered. In an apartment down in Greenwich Village. We're—we're looking into the circumstances."

I sound as if I were writing a report, Shapiro thought. "Circumstances surrounding the death of—"

"No use standing here in the sun," Karn said. "Somebody killed Jo-An? That's what you're saying."

Shapiro said yes, but he spoke to Karn's back. He walked after the shorter man between the white pillars and into the house. He heard the man in the white jacket taking something out of the Cadillac's trunk, but he did not look back. He went after Karn and through a wide entrance hall and, to the right, into a big living room with venetian blinds closed against the afternoon sun. Sunlight sifted between the slats and made patterns on a polished oak floor.

Oscar Karn walked down the long room, his golf shoes clattering a little on the floor and leaving marks on it. He walked toward a bar at the end of the room. Nathan Shapiro followed him halfway down the room and stopped.

At the bar, Karn turned back. He said, "You want a drink?"

"No."

"God knows I do," Karn said. "Sit down somewhere, will you?"

Shapiro found a chair facing a low sofa, with a table between the chair and the sofa. Karn brought a tall glass with ice and whisky in it and sat on the sofa. He said, "What did you say your name is? I'm no good at names. Particularly—well, when something like this is sprung on me. *God! Jo-An!*"

"Nathan Shapiro. I'm a lieutenant, Mr. Karn. Working out of Homicide, Manhattan South."

"Who'd kill a girl like her? Who'd want to?"

"We're trying to find out, Mr. Karn."

"Suppose you tell me about it, Lieutenant. And then I'll tell you anything I can. Anything you think might help."

Shapiro told him about it.

Karn said, "Jesus *Christ*." Then he said, "In an apartment way down there? Calling herself Jones?"

"Yes."

"You think she didn't kill herself? Not that I think she would have. Still—from the way you say it looked?"

"We don't think she killed herself, Mr. Karn," Shapiro said. "You knew she was in New York?"

"She came up to see us. Brought her manuscript with her. She'd sent along three, maybe four chapters in advance. I said, 'Come along and bring it with you.' She showed up five or six weeks ago."

"And did she—it was a new novel, I gather?"

"Yes. She called it 'Lonely Waters.' It was—from what I got to read of it, the best she'd done. They'll use the big words for it, Lieutenant. Words like 'great,' maybe."

"She gave you the manuscript?"

"No, she didn't. She'd decided there were things she wanted to do with it. Changes she wanted to make. She worked like that, getting everything right. She has—had it about ready, though. She was going to bring it in Monday at the latest. Possibly sooner."

"She told you that? When, Mr. Karn?"

"Tuesday, I think it was. Yes, it would have been last Tuesday."

"She came into your office and told you that? Or told you on the telephone?"

"Phone. I hadn't seen her for—oh, three weeks, at a guess."

"You knew she was in this Gay Street apartment?"

"No. I supposed she was staying at the Algonquin, where she'd stayed before. Working there."

"She didn't say anything about having rented a place in Gay Street? To work in, I suppose?"

"No. But—well, it's not an unusual thing for a writer to do, Lieutenant. Sort of—well, hide out. Get away from people.

From telephone calls, and friends coming in and that sort of thing."

"She had a telephone in the apartment," Shapiro said. "Do you know whether she had many friends in New York?"

"No. But—well, after that last book of hers she was pretty famous, Lieutenant. It would have got around she was in town and—well, people would have bothered her. Interrupting people. Some of them can write damn near any place. In a boiler factory, for all I know. Some of them have to go into cells to work. Jo-An's—Jo-An was—one of that kind. Interruptions threw her." He drank from his glass. He shook his head. He said, "*Damn*," and the word seemed to explode in his throat. He said, "Such a damned *waste*."

"You knew her pretty well, Mr. Karn?"

"Know all my writers pretty well. Reason they come to me. One of the reasons. The other is that I put them over. The way I did her."

"I want to know anything you can tell me about her," Shapiro said. "We can never tell what may help us. Things that wouldn't seem to have any relevance—well, sometimes they do. You say she was famous after this last book? The last one that was published, I mean."

"*Snake Country.* Yes. It was—well, what some people call a bombshell. After it started we had to bring out a new printing every month. Damn near every month, anyway. And after the movie came out, paperback went into millions."

"Probably made her a lot of money," Shapiro said.

"Made everybody a lot of money," Karn said. "This new one will too, from what I've seen of it."

"Which you say is only three or four chapters," Shapiro said. "Do you know where the rest of it is, Mr. Karn? The rest of the manuscript? That she was going to bring in Monday, or sooner?"

"In her hotel room," Karn said. "Or in this apartment you speak of. It's bound—"

He stopped abruptly. He looked over his glass at Nathan Shapiro.

"No," Shapiro said. "It isn't in either of those places, Mr.

Karn. Perhaps she changed her mind? Sent it to your company by mail?"

Karn's dark eyes narrowed. He started to shake his head and stopped the movement. He said, "I suppose it could just—just sit there a minute, will you, Lieutenant? Make yourself a drink if you like."

He got up. He went across the big room and out of it. Shapiro just sat there. He did not make himself a drink. Karn was gone for almost ten minutes. He started to speak as he came into the room. He said, "Damned if she didn't. Special delivery. It showed up at the office around two this afternoon. A hell of a big bundle of it, my secretary says."

He went to the table and picked his glass up and carried it back to the bar. He returned with it full.

"She never did that before," he said, after he had drunk from his glass. "A lot of them don't trust the mails. Think their manuscripts are—oh, priceless. Carry them around in their hands like—oh, like babies. Or make sure their agents do."

"Miss Lacey didn't have an agent?"

"What makes you say that? Assume that?"

"Why," Shapiro said, "because she seems to have sent this new manuscript direct to you. To the company, that is. You just said, didn't you, that some writers send in their books through their agents?"

"She didn't need an agent," Karn said. "Not with me, she didn't. Just be throwing away ten per cent of her money."

"Anyway," Shapiro said, "now you've got this new book of hers. You'll publish it, Mr. Karn?"

"We sure as hell will."

"After you merge with—what is the other publishing house, Mr. Karn?"

"Jefferson—what makes you think we're going to merge with anybody, Lieutenant?"

As he said that, Karn's voice grated more harshly than before.

"Just heard there was a rumor going around," Shapiro said. "We pick up a lot of rumors. Your company isn't going to merge with the Jefferson Press, then?"

60

"That have anything to do with Jo-An Lacey?"

"I shouldn't think so, Mr. Karn. Thing is, we never know what things may have to do with one another. Not in my trade, anyway. About this merger?"

"They made overtures. There's nothing definite. And it's supposed to be off the record, Shapiro."

"Things leak," Shapiro said. "We find out all the time that things leak. Helps sometimes. Sometimes it doesn't. Let's get back to Miss Lacey. You'd known her for some time, Mr. Karn?"

"About eight years. Since we published her first book. That was about eight years ago. Nice little job, but it didn't go. Some publishers would have let her slide when it didn't. Not Oscar Karn, Incorporated. Not the way I do business. Never has been. You come on somebody you think's going to be good and you stick with them. Nurse them along, you might say. Sometimes nothing comes of it. Sometimes—well, once in a thousand times a Jo-An Lacey comes of it."

"She's been with you for three books, somebody told me," Shapiro said. "The last one *Snake Country*, which was—what did you call it?—oh, a bombshell."

"That's right."

"Mind telling me how she happened to come to you in the first place, Mr. Karn? Come to you to be published, I mean of course?"

"She didn't," Karn said. "I went out and got her. Want to hear about that, Lieutenant? Can't see that it will help you, but it's no secret."

"We can't tell what will help," Shapiro said. "We just—well, sort of scratch around. To see what we can scratch up. Yes, Mr. Karn, I'd like to hear how Miss Lacey became a Karn author."

"Writer, she always called it. Thought the word 'author' was a stuffy word. They get odd notions, writers do. Wouldn't be writers if they didn't, I guess. Odd breed, writers are."

"I don't know much about writers," Shapiro said, in his sad voice. Any more, he thought, than I've known about painters and theater people and evangelists.

"An odd bunch," Karn said. "Well, about Jo-An—eight years

61

ago, and she was just a kid then, I happened to come on a short story she'd had in some Southern magazine. One of these special little magazines. You know what I mean."

It was a statement, assuming knowledge Nathan Shapiro didn't have. He didn't think it worthwhile to say so.

"Short piece," Karn said. "Sort of thing you'd pass over without thinking about ninety-nine times out of a hundred. Only, I didn't. I read it and then read it again and I thought, My God, here's a woman can write. So I got her address from this magazine and wrote her. Asked her if she had ever thought of writing a novel and whether she already had a publisher. Well—"

She had thought of writing a novel, Karn told Nathan Shapiro. In fact, she had one half written. No, she did not have a publisher. The story in the magazine was the first thing she'd ever had published. She'd just sent it in and it had been accepted and she had got paid twenty-five dollars.

"They don't pay anything, these little magazines," Karn said. "And a lot of kids are so excited about having something in print they don't care. Figure it makes them Writers with a capital W, if you know what I mean. So—"

Karn had written Jo-An Lacey in nethermost Alabama and asked her to send him what she had finished of the novel. She had sent him about a hundred pages. "She couldn't type worth a damn. The first twenty pages or so were single-spaced. Single-spaced, if you can believe."

Shapiro let appropriate disbelief show on his long sad face.

"But I read it," Karn said. "It was a kid's try. First hundred pages and no story line. And some of the dialogue was pretty bad. Sort of thing kids do when they've read a lot and—well, not listened enough to the way people talk. But all the same, the girl could write. She needed an editor. They all do, you know. But she had what it takes. Had—all right, had a hell of a lot of what it takes. So I flew down to Mobile."

He had flown down, he told Shapiro, and taken the hundred typescript pages with him. He had done some editing before he took off and did more on the plane. He had rented a car and driven out to "this plantation place."

"Big house," Karn said. "Tumbling down a good deal. Damn

it, the place has even got a ballroom. Picture that, will you? And a bunch of—well, you'd have to call them shacks—she told me had been slave quarters in her great-grandfather's time. Carries you back, doesn't it? And here was this pretty little kid living in this enormous old wreck with this brother of hers. And writing like an angel on a beat-up typewriter."

Karn paused and shook his head. Shapiro got a photograph out of his pocket. He said, "This is Miss Lacey, Mr. Karn?"

Karn looked at the photograph of a dead face. He looked at it for a long time. Then he put fingers against his forehead and, after almost as long a time, said, "Yes, Lieutenant. That's Jo-An. Taken after—after she was dead?"

"Yes," Shapiro said.

"She was so damned alive," Karn said. "Life sort of sparkled in her face."

"I know," Shapiro said. "They look different when they're dead. You talked to her about her book?"

Karn had talked to her about it; he had gone over it with her and made suggestions. "Mostly about the story line." He had told her he would buy the book when she finished it. "Oh, I said if it held up."

It had been about six months, he thought, before he received the manuscript. It had held up. "All right, I knew it wasn't going to be a world-beater. But I knew I wanted to grab her before somebody else did. So I sent along a contract."

The book, which had been called *Something to Remember*, had been published. It had got a "couple of all-right notices" and had sold a little over fifteen hundred copies. "Fifteen hundred and twenty-one," Karn said. "Figures like that stick in your mind, somehow. And we lost a bit of money, of course."

Karn said he could have dropped Jo-An Lacey then; he said that most publishers would have dropped her. "We're in the business to make money," Karn said. "You don't make money out of flops. But when you get the feel of a talent, a special talent in her case, you cut your losses and nurse it along. I do, anyway."

So he had encouraged the slight, pretty girl living in a mansion which was falling apart to write another novel. It had taken her two years to do it, but she sent it along, and Oscar Karn, Incorporated, had published it. It had done a little better than the first one, but not much better. "Something under three thousand. Not up to the break-even point for us, but what the hell? There's more to publishing than making money, Lieutenant. For me, anyway. All right, I know people in the business who'd have dropped her. I didn't. And what I got was *Snake Country*. And now this new one, which if it holds up—and I'm damned sure it will hold up—will be as good. Probably be better, with the reputation she's got now." He stopped and shook his head. "Had now, damn it," he said, more or less to himself.

"I suppose you have a contract with Miss Lacey," Shapiro said. "Something that will—oh, authorize you to publish this new one? I don't know much about how these things are arranged."

"Sure we have. You think we wouldn't tie her up? Because we played along with her, and lost money at it, doesn't mean we're soft in the head, Lieutenant."

"I never thought you were, Mr. Karn," Shapiro said. "The contract covers this new book, I take it?"

"Yes. I told you we're not soft—"

"I know you did," Shapiro said. "Somebody told me something about options. I'm not sure I understood about them. About a clause in an original contract which provides options on the next two books. Somebody said that was the usual practice."

"Who's this somebody?"

"I don't know that I remember, Mr. Karn. Somebody in town I was asking about Miss Lacey. This new book will be the fourth you've published by Miss Lacey."

"Are you trying to get at something, Lieutenant?"

"Just wondering. Trying to get things straightened out in my own mind. I mean, with Miss Lacey dead, she can't sign a new contract, of course."

"Her estate can. Which will mean this brother of hers. As a matter of fact—"

He broke off. Shapiro waited.

"Nothing that would interest you, Lieutenant," Karn said,

after the pause had extended. "You can take it for granted we'll publish 'Lonely Waters.'"

Shapiro said, "All right, Mr. Karn." Then he added, "I take it that will be true whether you go in with this other firm or not? Merge with it?"

"That's still just talk. Lawyers' talk. Nothing may come of it. Look, Lieutenant—"

Shapiro said, "Yes?"

"I want to do anything I can to help. But we *have* got people coming for cocktails. Too late to put them off. I'd like to, with this happening to Jo-An. But—"

He looked down at his heavy golf shoes. He looked at his slacks, which had a grass stain on them.

"Couple more questions," Shapiro said. "Then I'll get out of the way, Mr. Karn. I appreciate the time you've given me already."

Karn emptied his glass, with finality. But he said, "Go ahead, Lieutenant Shapiro."

"You met Miss Lacey for the first time when you flew down to Alabama," Shapiro said. "You met her after that? I mean, got to know her?"

"She brought the second book up herself," Karn said. "I went over it with her. I was editing her myself. Also—well, she was here almost a week that time. I showed her around the city a little. She'd never been here before. Never been out of Alabama, probably. It's quite a city for a kid to see, Lieutenant."

"Yes," Shapiro said. "Since she's been here this time. With this new manuscript. You've seen something of her?"

"Took her to lunch a few times. To dinner once, I think. Oh, I brought her out here once to meet Mrs. Karn. And to see how we live in the country up here."

"But you never knew—I mean she never told you—about having an apartment in Gay Street."

"No. I told you that. But there was nothing strange about that. She wanted a place to work, was all."

Shapiro stood up. He again thanked Mr. Karn for the time he had spared. Karn stood up, too.

"Oh," Shapiro said, "one other thing. This time you took her

65

to dinner, Mr. Karn? Was it down in Greenwich Village? They say there are some good restaurants down there."

"I took her to the Plaza," Karn said. "It was—well, just a place she'd heard about."

Karn went across the living room with Shapiro and through the entrance hall. He stood in the open doorway while Shapiro walked to the police car. The Cadillac wasn't there any more. Shapiro assumed it had been put in the garage.

It took him less time to drive back to New York than it had taken him to drive to Mount Kisco. People were driving out of the city for weekends in the country. Not many were driving into it.

He turned the car in at West Twentieth Street and, after finding that Anthony Cook had checked out at the end of his shift, took the subway home to Brooklyn.

Nathan opened the door of the apartment and said, "Hi," into it. Cleo, the Scottie bitch, made excited sounds, followed by a thump. She had been on a chair she wasn't supposed to be on. Everything was in order. Cleo rushed to him and tried to climb his right leg and he scratched her behind the ears. Rose said "Hi" from the kitchen and came into the living room and stood in front of her husband and looked up into his face. A small line came between her dark eyebrows.

Everything was in order.

"You're tired," Rose Shapiro said.

"No, dear," Nathan said. "Just puzzled. This time it's writers and publishers and something called an agent."

"Take your gun off and sit down," Rose told him. "I'll bring you something long and cold. Summer's come, Nathan."

"Just a little—" Nathan Shapiro said, but Rose was already on her way to the kitchen. He took his gun off and put it on the shelf it lives on when it is not living on Shapiro. He sat down. Rose must have got home earlier than usual. She had turned the air conditioner on. He stretched out his legs and looked at his feet. Then he looked up at the portrait hanging over the fireplace—the portrait of Rabbi Emmanuel Shapiro, his father. The dark eyes of the portrait held, Nathan thought, the sadness of Nathan's own. Rabbi Shapiro had worn a beard.

This Oscar Karn wears a beard, Shapiro thought. So does this writer named Shepley. There are too many beards around, to say nothing of too many writers.

Rose brought two tall glasses in on a tray. There was ice in both of them. The liquid in one of them might have been water—water with bubbles in it. The other liquid was red. There were bubbles in it, too.

Rose put the two glasses down on the long table in front of the sofa and picked up her gin and tonic. She held it toward Nathan's glass and they clicked glasses together. They sipped from the glasses. Rose had diluted Nathan's sweet wine with ice and soda, which proved that summer had come.

"After all," Rose Shapiro said, "writers are people too, Nathan. It's this girl in the Village? It was on the radio, except on the radio it was suicide."

"No," Nathan said. "I'm afraid it wasn't, dear. And Bill Weigand should have put somebody else on it."

"Of course," Rose said, consolation in her soft voice. There was, however, the trace of a smile on her gentle lips.

7

Because it wasn't to be one of the good evenings, there wasn't any hurry. Tony Cook walked home to Twelfth Street from Twentieth. The sun was still high and it was warming up. Tomorrow, he thought, will be muggy. Tomorrow we'll all be choking on the air.

He climbed the flight of stairs to his apartment and went into it and turned the window air conditioner on. He showered, ending with a jet of cold which made him jump. He shaved, although he had shaved that morning. And although he wasn't doing anything this evening which would need a smoothly shaven face. He made himself a drink and sat, wearing only shorts, waiting for the room to cool and wondering what he would do with the evening.

For a long time, Tony thought, there wasn't any real problem about evenings. Off-duty evenings were—oh, hit or miss. Mostly, he thought, I'd hit on something. I'd call up a girl and take her to dinner and see what else, if anything, came of it. Or if the first girl was tied up, I'd call a second girl. Or, more often I suppose, I'd go to a movie. Or look at television. Or just sit around and read and go to bed early. Off-duty evenings were something which, in one way or another, could be counted on to take care of themselves. Sometimes I'd even bowl. Evenings used to be haphazard, but usually they turned out all right. Not special, mostly, but all right.

And now, because, a while back, a very tall and deceptively lean girl walked into a studio and tried to steal a picture a dead painter had done, evenings aren't the way they used to be. Now they're either special or empty. This was an empty one. It's a hell of a note, Tony thought. It's really one hell of a note.

I could call her, Tony thought. Maybe today didn't turn out to be as rough as she thought it would be. Maybe I could, anyway, take her to dinner. She's still got to eat, even if she's tired out. I could give her a ring. That wouldn't do any harm.

He reached out a hand toward the telephone. But then he drew the hand back. She'd say no, and when she said no she meant it. If she were home at all, she'd probably be taking a shower. He could see her under the shower, with water running down her body. She wasn't lean at all, really, when you got a good look at her. A lot of people did get a good look, of course. Too damn—

Tony grabbed his mind and turned it around. I'm going a little nuts, he thought. It's her way of making a living and that's her business. I don't own the girl. Ownership doesn't come into it and never will, because we don't want it that way. I'll just—

He got up and made himself another drink. I'll finish this one, he thought, and get dressed and go out and have dinner some place. Maybe I'll go to André's and see if this man named Lorenzo has remembered anything more about a beard. Anyway, I'll get some of that damned good lasagna.

It was getting cooler in the room. Tony turned on the television set. Cronkite was already on. Tony hadn't realized it was that late. No more hell seemed to be breaking loose than usual. The administration was up to some new trick or other and CBS didn't seem to think much of it. Come to that, Tony Cook didn't either, for what difference that made. Somebody ought to send somebody a telegram about it.

Tony finished his drink and cut the television off and dressed to go out to dinner. He put on one of the striped shirts he had begun to wear because Rachel liked striped shirts on him. He put his gun on, and slacks and a summer jacket cut so that the gun didn't show unless you were looking for it. He thought, Charles is nearer than André's, but it costs more. And anyway, it's not a place to go alone. And Rachel and I were there last night. Maybe tomorrow night we'll go uptown.

He opened the apartment door and made sure it was locked behind him—locked with the special lock he'd had put on. Of course, the lock wouldn't outlast a real pro, but it would delay him some, which was about all you could expect.

While he was making sure the door was fast, he heard footfalls on the stairs above him. They were heavy, a man's steps. He looked up the stairs; Laurence Shepley was coming down them. Halfway down the flight to the third floor, Shepley said, "Hi, neighbor." He sounded, Tony thought, like a man who had had a couple of drinks. Tony said, "Evening, Mr. Shepley," and thought that he probably sounded like a man who had had a couple of drinks.

Shepley said, "'Constabulary duty to be done,' Mr. Cook?"

"Even policemen have to eat," Cook told him, and Shepley came on down the stairs.

"Yes," Shepley said. "People have to eat. Whatever happens. People get killed and still people have to eat. Or, anyway, try to." He stopped beside Tony Cook on the landing. "You going to Charles? Where you were last night with that tall girl?"

"No," Tony said. "Not tonight. A place on down a ways. Place called André's. Italian food. You ever been there, Mr. Shepley?"

"No. Good place?"

"I like it. Want to come along and see if you do?"

"Keeping me under your eye, Detective Cook?"

He said it pleasantly, as if it were a joke.

"Nothing like that," Tony said. "Why would I?"

"Because I knew a young woman named Jo-An Lacey," Shepley said. "And because she's dead. Are you meeting somebody at this restaurant? That lieutenant you were teamed up with today?"

"Nobody," Tony said. "Come along, if you like. Only probably you've got a date."

"No. I haven't got a date. Not—well, not a night for dates." He shook his head. "Keep thinking of Jo-An," he said. "Seems —well, it seems such a goddamn waste, somehow. Yes, I'll come along to this Italian place."

They went on down the stairs. They walked east and south for half a dozen blocks. André's Restaurant was in the basement of a narrow, four-story building. They went down the stairs into it, Tony going first. A black-haired man in a dark suit met them inside and said, "Gentlemen? Two?" Then he said, "Oh, good evening, Mr. Cook. Table in the garden, maybe?"

He looked at the man with the red beard. There was nothing in his face to suggest he had ever seen him before. Nothing, anyway, that Tony Cook could see. Tony said that a table in the garden would be fine. He looked at Shepley and said, "O.K. with you?"

"Wherever you say. You know the place."

It was moderately cool in the garden beyond the bar and the inside tables, few of which were occupied. In the center of the garden there was a small fountain, but it was only a trickle of a fountain. The table they were taken to was beside precisely trimmed green bushes. "A cocktail before dinner, gentlemen?"

Tony said, "Bourbon on the rocks, please." Shepley said, "Very dry martini. Up." The waiter said, "Gentlemen," and went away.

Shepley had said almost nothing as they walked down from West Twelfth Street. Tony had been thinking about Rachel and warning himself not to get possessive about her. He was still surprised, and chagrined, at the sudden spurt of almost anger in his mind when he thought of the many men who had a good look at her as she practiced her profession.

"She was a damn sweet kid," Shepley said. "And a hell of a good writer. Her brother called me up this afternoon. And came around to—"

The waiter said, "Gentlemen," and put drinks on the table

in front of them. He said, "Would you care to order now, gentlemen?"

"Later," Tony said. The waiter said, "Whenever you're ready, gentlemen," and went away. Tony looked across the table at the red-bearded Laurence Shepley, and when he spoke he spoke very slowly.

"Her brother?" Tony Cook said. "Called you and then came to see you? *You.* Why you, Mr. Shepley?"

"Said he was her brother," Shepley said. "Said he'd gone to her apartment and rung the bell and got no answer. Said she had written him something about having seen me a few times. And that he didn't know anybody in town and thought I might know where she was. All right, that's what he said."

"Just because she'd mentioned you in a letter?"

"What he said."

"What did you tell him, Shepley?"

"What could I tell him? That she was dead. I tried—well, tried to make it easy. But there's no making it easy, is there?"

"How she came to die? Did you tell him that?"

"Not at first. At first I said there'd been an accident. But—well, he apparently didn't buy that. Asked if he could come around and see me and I said yes, he could."

"You didn't tell him to get in touch with us? With the police?"

"Not on the telephone. When he came around, yes, I did. And that the police seemed to think—well, that somebody had killed her. You want to hear all of it, Cook?"

Shepley drank from his glass. Tony had left his untouched. Now he raised it and drank from it. Then he said, "Yes. I want to hear all of it."

"He had a suitcase with him. Lugged it all the way upstairs. He said, 'What's happened to Sis?' I said that she had been found dead in her apartment. That the police had taken over. That he had better get in touch with the police, because that was all I knew about it."

"He'd gone to the Gay Street apartment? Knew she was living there as a Miss Jones?"

"Yes. I suppose she'd written him. He was—he was all broken

72

up. Kept saying, 'It can't be Sis. Can't be Jo-An.' That sort of thing. I gave him a drink, but it didn't seem to help much."

"You're sure he was her brother?"

"How could I be? He said he was her brother. He said, 'I'm John Henry Lacey, Jo-An's brother.' That was when he first telephoned me. He said, 'Do you know where she might be, Mr. Shepley? Because something she wrote me made me think she might be in trouble. Need help.' He talked—well, the way she talked, only more so. Very Southern accent. And damn if he didn't look like Old South when he showed up. Tall, rather thin, blond hair. And blond chin whiskers. You know? The goatee kind of thing."

Shepley absently stroked his own trimmed beard.

"He looked," Shepley said, "as if he'd been brought up on mint juleps. As if he ought to be called 'Colonel.' "

Tony gave that the moderate smile it warranted. He said, "When you told him to go to the police did he say he would?"

"Said something about its being an idea. He didn't commit himself."

"You didn't tell him where to go? To what station house, I mean?"

"I don't know myself."

Tony said that Charles Street would be the best place, but he said it absently. He finished his drink and pushed his chair back. "When the waiter comes back," Tony said, "will you order another round for me? I won't be long."

He went out of the garden and into the restaurant. The headwaiter was doubling as bartender. Tony went to the bar. He said, "The man I came in with, Larry. You ever see him before? The one with the beard?"

Lorenzo shrugged his shoulders, very thoroughly. He said, "Everybody's asking about beards. What's about beards?"

"Everybody?"

"Well, Pieronelli. From the precinct squad. You know Charley?"

"Yes."

"Wanted to know if this girl who got killed ever came in here. I told him—"

73

"I know what you told him, Larry. Any chance this man who came in with me is the man who came in with her? The man with the beard?"

Lorenzo shrugged again.

"Look," he said, "I told Charley all I knew was the man had a beard. Lots of men have beards."

"A beard like this man with me has? Or, maybe, a chin beard? You know. What they call a goatee. Used to, anyway."

"Because like a goat," Lorenzo said. "I'm sorry, Mr. Cook. Just a beard. Could be it was a little beard like a goat's. Could be it was like this man's you came in with. Like I told Charley, it was just a beard."

Tony went to a telephone booth. Nobody who said he was John Henry Lacey had showed up at Charles Street. He dialed again. Nobody who said he was John Henry Lacey, brother of Jo-An Lacey, had showed up at Homicide, Manhattan South. Tony thought for a moment or two. Probably Nathan Shapiro would be in the middle of dinner. What was it Shepley had said part of? Of course. "'A policeman's lot is not a happy one.'" Tony dialed a Brooklyn number. A woman answered him.

"Rose," Tony Cook said, "I'm sorry as hell. This is Tony. Nate handy?"

Rose said, "A minute, Tony," and it was less than a minute.

Tony told Nathan Shapiro about the man who said he was the brother of Jo-An Lacey.

Shapiro said, "Mmmm." He said, "Why go to Shepley?"

"Apparently the girl had mentioned Shepley in a letter or something. What he told Shepley. What Shepley says he told him."

Shapiro said "Mmmm" again.

Tony said, "Yeah."

"You say he has a beard?"

"What Shepley says. A little one."

"He'd just got into town? From what he told Shepley?"

"He had a suitcase with him. Lugged it up to Shepley's apartment. From what Shepley says. Went around to his sister's apartment and didn't find her. I didn't get very far with Shepley. I thought I ought to check in."

"Didn't show up at precinct," Shapiro said. "Or at our squad room. Headquarters, maybe?"

Tony said he hadn't checked on that yet.

"Might as well," Shapiro said. "Incidentally, Miss Lacey's manuscript seems to have shown up. Karn thinks he's got a right to publish it. Or says that's what he thinks. That the estate will have the right to sign a contract. This brother could be the estate, couldn't he?"

"Mobile doesn't know, offhand anyway, of any other Laceys kicking around."

"Keep after Shepley. See if this brother said he'd just got in. You're supposed to be off tomorrow, aren't you?"

The word "supposed" was the key word—a key which was going to lock Tony Cook in on the job. Tony said, "Yes. That's the schedule."

"So was I," Shapiro said. There was a sigh in his voice. Of course, there usually was. "I'll see you in the morning," Shapiro said.

"Sure," Tony said.

Shapiro sighed again.

"This man Karn," he said. "This publisher of hers. He's got a beard too, Tony."

Tony said, "Oh."

"Yes," Shapiro said. "In the morning, then. You might check headquarters. Place out-of-towners would go, probably. Where are you now, Tony?"

Tony told Nathan Shapiro where he was. He told Shapiro that Jo-An Lacey probably had been at the same restaurant once or twice. And that she had been there with a man who wore a beard. And that the man who ran André's couldn't identify Shepley, "who's here with me," as the man with the beard.

"Identifications are wobbly things at best," Nathan told him, needlessly. "Unless this brother shows up, I'll see you in the morning."

"If he does?"

"I'll see you tonight," Nathan Shapiro said, and hung up.

Tony called headquarters. It took longer. There was no record that a man calling himself John Henry Lacey the Third had been around to inquire about his sister.

Tony's bourbon was on the garden table when he got back to it. Shepley had half finished another martini. Shepley said, "I'm getting ahead of you."

Tony started to catch up, but he didn't hurry about it.

"I was talking to the lieutenant," Tony said. "He wanted me to ask you whether this man who said he was Lacey told you how long he'd been in town."

"I don't remem—wait a minute. He said something about just having got off the train. I'm pretty sure he said train. And he did have this suitcase with him. Way he handled it, I thought it was heavy. Wondered why he hadn't left it downstairs."

"The wicked city," Tony said. "Afraid somebody would steal it. Come to that, somebody might have. He said train, as you remember it?"

"Yes. Surprised me a little. Probably why I remember it. I didn't know they were still running trains."

"A few, I guess. You going to have another?"

"Probably," Shepley said. "It's been—well, sort of a bad day. Maybe I was fonder of Jo-An than I realized."

Tony finished his drink and ordered lasagna. Shepley ordered another drink and then said, "O.K., I'll try the lasagna too."

Shepley didn't eat all of his lasagna. He pushed his plate away and said he thought he'd have a brandy, and would Tony join him? Tony Cook said he thought he wouldn't; said he had to go uptown and make a telephone call. He drank espresso and, for a moment or two, watched Shepley sip cognac. Then he stood up.

"That's right," Shepley said. "Thanks for putting me onto this place, Cook. I may stick around a while."

Tony left Shepley sticking around. Tony got a cab and went up to West Twentieth Street.

It was a little after eight by his watch. In Mobile, Alabama,

76

it would be—would be what? An hour earlier, at a guess. Lieutenant Buncombe, Mobile police force, might conceivably be on duty.

Buncombe was. In answer to Tony's question, he said he didn't know, but he could guess. Old man Sturdevant, probably. He handled most of the old-timers because he was an old-timer himself. Leslie Sturdevant, that would be. But he wouldn't be at his office; not at this hour of a Friday night. His club, could be. Sold his plantation after his wife died and the children moved away. All right, suh, he'd get the number if Mistuh Cook was sure he wanted it.

"The old man won't like it," Buncombe said. "He's a crusty old so-and-so. Being pretty well along, as you might say."

But here it was, and Tony wrote it down. He hung up and dialed the number. He was costing the New York Police Department money in telephone tolls. The call went south and west across the country, with clicking sounds and irrelevant voices. Finally, a voice said, "The Plantation Club, suh."

"Is Mr. Sturdevant—Mr. Leslie Sturdevant—in the club?"

"I believe so, suh. But he probably is at dinner."

Tony said he would like to speak to Mr. Sturdevant. He added that he was calling from New York. He told the Plantation Club who was calling. The Plantation Club did not seem unduly impressed.

"I shall see if Mr. Sturdevant is in the club, suh. And whether he will wish to speak to you."

Tony waited. He waited for some minutes. Then he heard, "This is Leslie Sturdevant." The voice was high; it was an old voice.

"This is Detective Anthony Cook, New York Police, sir. Sorry if I've interrupted your dinner."

There was no answer to this.

"We thought you might be able to help us, sir."

"In what connection?"

"I've been told you may be the legal representative of Miss Jo-An Lacey, Mr. Sturdevant. Miss Lacey is—"

"Miss Lacey is dead," Sturdevant said. "It was in the news-

77

papers. According to the account, Miss Lacey committed suicide. Most surprising. Most shocking."

"We've reason to think it wasn't suicide, sir. Did you represent her?"

"My firm has always represented the Laceys, Mr. Cook. When they needed representation."

"Did you draw up a will for Miss Lacey, sir?"

"Mr. Cook, I am now at my club. Having dinner with friends. Business matters are transacted at my office. It is unlikely that I will care to discuss the affairs of my clients. If you like, you can telephone me at my office on Monday. Good—"

"Wait just a moment, Mr. Sturdevant. You can tell me one thing. Did Miss Lacey leave a will?"

"The records, sir. The records are at my office. I do not bring them with me when I visit my club. In any event, it would be a matter for my associates. Good—"

"The matter is rather urgent, Mr. Sturdevant. I don't expect you to have the details of the will at—at your fingertips. But surely you know whether a will was drawn up for her by your office."

"The relationship between lawyer and client is privileged, Mr. Cook. In Alabama, at any rate."

The man was ancient, Tony thought—ancient and stately. You have to take them as they come.

"Everywhere, far's I know," Tony said. "It's a very simple question, Mr. Sturdevant. I can't see that any breach of confidence is involved. Did Miss Lacey make a will, to your knowledge?"

There was a longish pause.

"I have no knowledge that she did," Sturdevant said in his high, old voice. "Of course, one of my associates may have taken care of the legal formalities."

"If one had, you would have been informed, sir?"

"I presume so."

"And were not, I gather. Which would mean she died intestate. Leaving considerable property."

"I have no knowledge of her financial situation, Mr. Cook. I assume that she may have profited considerably from this—

this rather unpleasant book of hers. But I have no personal knowledge."

"If she died—was killed, we think—without leaving a will, her next of kin would inherit?"

"Yes."

"That being?"

"Really, Cook. I suggest you call my office on—"

"On Monday," Cook said: "I'm afraid it's a little more pressing than that. Her brother?"

"She had a brother," Sturdevant admitted. The admission seemed somewhat to pain him. "Mr. John Henry Lacey the Third. His grandfather was for some years governor of our state, Mr. Cook."

"Her brother would be next of kin?"

"I cannot say that of my own knowledge. Call my office Monday and—"

"But he might be, Mr. Sturdevant?"

"Certainly. Now, if you will excuse me, sir? The gentlemen with whom I am dining are my guests."

"Of course, Mr. Sturdevant," Tony said. "Thanks for giving me so much of your time."

And so little else, Tony thought as he hung up. Lawyers are cagy birds. The old guy might, conceivably, come up with a will. Meanwhile—

A uniformed patrolman came into the squad room. He looked around it and came to Tony's desk.

"Man downstairs wants to see whoever's in charge of the Lacey case," he said. "That be you, Cook?"

"The lieutenant," Cook said. "But—yeah, I'm working with him. Give you a name, this man?"

"Lacey," the patrolman said. "John Henry Lacey Third. Something like that."

"Send him up," Cook said and then, "No. Give me five minutes or so, huh?"

The patrolman said, "Sure." Tony dialed a Brooklyn telephone number.

8

The man who came to the doorway of the squad room and stood in it and looked around the room—looked at desks and men at some of them pounding typewriters—was pretty much as Shepley had said he was. He was tall and spare; he had thinning blond hair and rather sparse chin whiskers. He was wearing a seersucker suit. Tony stood up at his desk and beckoned, and the tall man came to the desk. He held out his hand and Tony took it.

"I am John Henry Lacey," the man said. "You're in charge of this awful thing about Sis?"

"Not in charge," Tony said. "Helping out. Lieutenant Shapiro's in charge."

Lacey repeated, "Shapiro?" as if he didn't much like the sound of it. "I asked to see whoever is in charge. Somebody told me you think my sister was murdered."

"The lieutenant's on his way over," Tony said. "Yes, we're afraid Miss Lacey was murdered. We don't know by whom, Mr. Lacey. We'd appreciate—"

"She shouldn't have come up here," Lacey said. "She didn't belong here. It's no place for a Southern lady to come to."

Tony managed to believe his ears. It was a little difficult. This was only partly because of the depth of Lacey's Southern accent.

"It's a shocking thing to have happened," Tony said. "We're all sympathetic, Mr. Lacey. Realize the shock it is to you."

"Very well," Lacey said. "What are you going to do about it? You're one of the detectives, I guess."

"Yes," Tony said. "Anthony Cook. The lieutenant suggested we use his office until he gets here. What we're going to do about it, Mr. Lacey, is find out who killed your sister."

He went toward the corridor which leads to Nathan Shapiro's small office. Lacey hesitated for a moment. Then he followed Tony Cook. Tony sat at Nathan Shapiro's desk and gestured toward a chair opposite it and Lacey sat down on the chair. The light from the room's single, small, and not very clean window was on his face.

"As I understand it," Tony said, "you got into town—this afternoon, was it?"

"This afternoon. Yes."

"And went to your sister's apartment. Have any trouble finding Gay Street, Mr. Lacey? It's a little out of the way."

"The taxi driver found it. Probably drove me all over town to run up the fare, but he found it. Run-down little place. All crowded together like."

"The city's crowded together," Cook said. "You rang your sister's doorbell and didn't get an answer and then telephoned a man named Shepley. That's right?"

"My sister'd written me about meeting this Shepley," Lacey said. "Seemed to be seeing quite a bit of him. I thought he might know where she'd got to."

"Did she expect you, Mr. Lacey? Know you were coming?"

"Wrote her I was. Didn't say exactly when because I had a deal on. Didn't know when I'd get away. I'm in real estate back home."

"Any special reason for coming up to see her? I mean, had she asked you to or anything like that?"

"Damn it all, man, she was my sister. Worried me to have her way up here by herself, with no man to take care of her."

"You thought she needed taking care of?"

"Seems like she did, don't it? Seems like I should have come along sooner, don't it? No place for a lady to be by herself.

81

Probably was one of these long-haired bastards, wasn't it? Get them down home some, telling us how to run our business. About nigras, specially. Outside agitators. That's what they are."

"Did something she wrote you make you worried about her? Make you think she needed help?"

"Not out and out. I just got to thinking, and it seemed to me she was upset about something. Only she didn't write me that. Talked to her on the phone. So I figured I'd better come up."

Tony said he saw. He said, "She'd been in New York before, Mr. Lacey. Nothing happened to her. Were you worried about her when she was up here before?"

"When she was up here before, she was staying at a hotel. And Mr. Karn was showing her the town, I guess. Some hotel with sort of an Indian name."

"The Algonquin?"

"Sounds like it. But this time she had this little apartment. In Green-witch Village, she said it was. I just didn't like the sound of it. I'd heard about this Green-witch Village place. Communists all over the place, from what I'd heard. Anarchists, maybe. Not the kind of place a Southern lady ought to be living in."

"That was all? She didn't say anything that made you think she was afraid? Of something specific? Or someone specific? Or that she was depressed about something?"

"Can't say she did, mister. Just got worried about her. She's my sister. Only kinfolk she had."

"There aren't any other Laceys?"

"Nope. Just Sis and me. Used to be a lot of us around, but not any more."

"Are you married, Mr. Lacey?"

"No. Just never got around to it. What makes you ask a thing like that? Thought you were trying to catch whoever it was killed Sis."

Just wondering about the continuation of the Laceys, Tony thought, but did not say. Lacey, at a guess, was in his late forties. Fifteen years or so older than his sister had been. If he was going to do anything about the continuation of the Laceys it was time to get around to it.

"Habit we have in an investigation like this," Tony said. "Try to find out all we can about everybody concerned. Where are you staying, Mr. Lacey?"

"Expected to stay with Sis, of course. Natural thing to do, being she's my sister. But then I got this letter from Mr. Karn. Said since I was coming up he'd got me a room at some hotel or other. Don't know why, seeing Sis had this apartment."

"It's a small apartment," Tony said. "She couldn't have put you up there. Anyway, it's sealed now, until we're finished with it. What hotel, Mr. Lacey?"

"Got it here somewhere," Lacey said, and felt in a pocket of the seersucker jacket. Then he felt in the other pocket and took a slip of paper out of it.

"The Algonquin, it says," Lacey said, "same place Sis stayed last time she was up here in New York. Know where that might be, mister?"

"Yes," Tony said. "Uptown a ways. Very good old hotel. Famous, actually. Have you checked in there yet?"

"No. Went to see this man Shepley. Man with a lot of beard. Couldn't tell me anything. So I found a place and had something to eat. Can't eat on trains. Didn't have any grits this place I went to. Funny place, not having any grits."

"You'd probably have to go up to Harlem to find grits," Tony said.

"Nigras up there, from what I heard. Don't eat with nigras. Where's this lieutenant of yours? Shapiro? That's what you said?"

"Nathan Shapiro."

"Sounds sort of like a Jew to me."

"He is, Mr. Lacey. And a damn fine person. And a damn good policeman."

"If you say so," Lacey said, with no conviction in his voice. "Point is, where is he? We sit here chewing the fat and not getting anywhere I can see. Not finding out who killed—"

Nathan Shapiro came into his small office. Tony got up from the chair behind the desk and Shapiro sat down on it.

"Mr. Lacey, Lieutenant," Tony said. "Got worried about his sister and came up to—er—take care of her. Mr. Karn's got him a room at the Algonquin, he tells me."

Nathan Shapiro nodded his head. He looked, gloomily, at John Henry Lacey III. He said, "A very sad ending to your trip, Mr. Lacey."

Lacey said it sure was. Tony Cook sat down on the third chair in the little office.

"You say Mr. Karn got you a room?" Shapiro said. "When was that? The Mr. Karn is Oscar Karn, I suppose? Your late sister's publisher."

"That's the man. Oscar Karn, Incorporated. Oscar Karn, President. What it said on the letter. Got the letter last Tuesday."

"That would be the twentieth," Shapiro said. "And the letter said?"

"Said Sis had told him I might be coming up. And that he'd taken the liberty—that's the way he put it—of engaging me a room at this Algonquin place. Only he said Sis was staying there. But she wasn't. She was in this apartment down in something called Gay Street."

"She had an apartment in Gay Street," Shapiro said. "She also had a room at the Algonquin. In Gay Street, she called herself Jones. She didn't write you that?"

"Not that. Later—she called me on the phone. Wait a minute. She did say something about she'd rented the apartment from somebody called Jones. Said it would say 'Jones' on the doorbell. Called it a sub something."

"Sublet, probably," Shapiro said. "She seems to have been using the apartment as a place to work in. On the manuscript of her new book. You knew she was working on a new novel, Mr. Lacey?"

"Always was. Typewriter going all the time, pretty near. Didn't take the time, mostly, to get us anything to eat. Have to go down the road a piece to get a halfway decent meal, part of the time. Always at that typewriter of hers."

"She made money at it," Shapiro said. "You're in the real estate business, I understand. Profitable business?"

84

"I don't see what that's got to do with you, Shapiro."

"Probably nothing," Shapiro said. "Let's just say I'm curious. Have to be in my business, you know. Profitable, this real estate operation?"

"I make out. A little slow right now, maybe. But I make out."

"Fine," Shapiro said. "When your sister came up here, Mr. Lacey. Happen to know what she brought with her? I mean, her typewriter? Things like that? A rather bulky package of manuscript?"

"I guess so. I didn't much notice."

"You drove her to the airport? When she left to come up here, I mean. Helped her with her luggage?"

"Not the airport. The railroad station. Yeah, I drove her into town. Helped with her things. Yeah, I remember now. She had this typewriter with her. And a couple of suitcases. Pretty heavy, one of them was. I don't remember any bundle."

"Probably in the heavy suitcase," Shapiro said. "Do you happen to know whether your sister had made her will, Mr. Lacey?"

"I don't know for sure. Shouldn't think so. She was just a kid, really. Kids don't make wills. Never made one myself, matter of fact. And Sis was a lot younger than I am."

Shapiro said he saw. He said, "I suppose you and your sister had—have—a good many relations down in your part of the country?"

"Kinfolk," Lacey said. "No. Funny thing, because down our way folks usually have kin all over. Oh, I suppose a few cousins and the like. We didn't keep in touch much. Until the last few years we weren't up to entertaining much."

"Until your sister started to make money with her books," Shapiro said. "Any idea how much money, Mr. Lacey?"

"Don't rightly see what you're getting at, Shapiro," Lacey said. "I didn't do her bookkeeping. She had her own bank account, just like I had mine. This got something to do with who killed her? If somebody did kill her, that is."

"Somebody killed her," Shapiro said. "There's a term lawyers use, Mr. Lacey. *Cui bono.* Means 'for whose benefit.' Who stands to gain? If she left no will, you'd inherit, obviously, being her only near kin. If she did leave a will, would you be her heir then too?"

"Be up to her, wouldn't it?"

"Yes. Your sister wasn't married, I suppose?"

"No. And she wouldn't sneak off and get married without telling me, if that's what you're getting at." He paused for a second. He said, "Shapiro," with something like a snarl in his voice.

Shapiro seemed not to notice the snarl. But then Lacey stood up and Shapiro stood up with him.

"I don't have to sit here and answer damn-fool questions," Lacey said.

"No," Shapiro told him. "I'd supposed you'd want to help. But no. You'll probably want to check in at your hotel. I'll have a car run you up, if you like."

"I'll get there by myself," Lacey said. "Call up and get a taxi or something."

"You'll probably be able to pick a cab up on the street," Shapiro told him. "Free cabs have a light on on their roofs. Or, Tony, you might see Mr. Lacey gets out all right? Gets a cab to take him to the Algonquin? Easy to get lost in a strange city."

Tony said, "Sure, Lieutenant."

He led the way through the squad room and down the stairs. Lacey had left his suitcase at the precinct desk. Tony had no trouble in flagging down a cab. When the cab, with its driver instructed as to destination, pulled away from the curb, a black Plymouth with a man in a sports jacket at the wheel pulled away after it. Tony went back upstairs.

"On his way," Tony said. "With company to see he doesn't get lost."

Nathan Shapiro nodded his head. He said it was interesting that Oscar Karn had engaged a room for John Henry Lacey.

"The Third," Tony Cook said.

"The Third," Shapiro repeated. "There are a good many things interesting about Mr. Karn." He told Tony some of the things that, in Mount Kisco or near it, had interested him about Oscar Karn.

86

"He thinks he has the rights to this new book of hers?" Tony said. "And that the manuscript's been mailed to his office?"

"That's what he said."

"Could be there was fine print in the old contract," Tony said. "Could be the girl didn't read the fine print and—"

He stopped because Nathan was sadly moving his head from side to side.

"You're getting forgetful," Shapiro said. "This man Morton—the man who thought he was going to be her agent—had a look at her old contract. Got her a new one with another publisher. I don't think he'd have forgotten to read fine print, Tony. Unless, say, Karn has some sort of agreement, with her signature on it, making him her—I don't know what it would be." He sighed his frustration. "I'm the wrong man for this sort of thing. Bill ought to have realized that."

"Come off it," Tony said, speaking not as a detective to a lieutenant but as friend to friend. "Literary executor, maybe. Heard somebody at a party downtown talking about that sort of thing once."

"Could be," Shapiro said. "You go to very many parties with writers at them?"

"Some," Tony said. "Rachel knows a lot of people like that. Writers. Painters. People who write music. Sometimes I tag along with her."

Shapiro said, "Mmmm."

"I talked to a man in Mobile," Tony said. "A man named Sturdevant. The Laceys' lawyer. He admitted that much. Cagy old guy. But if she made a will he doesn't know about it. Says he doesn't, anyway."

"Yes," Shapiro said. "We have to go on what people say. At the start, anyway. No idea what kind of an estate she left, I suppose? And wouldn't—"

The telephone on his desk interrupted him. He said, "Shapiro." He listened. He said, "O.K. Suppose you stick around for an hour or so and see if he stays there." He hung up.

"Lacey's checked in at the Algonquin," Shapiro said. "And wouldn't tell you if he did have."

87

"No," Tony said. "Oh, that I can call him Monday at his office. I got hold of him at his club. Crusty about that."

"She had upwards of ten thousand in a checking account," Shapiro said. "I took a look at her checkbook in her room at the Algonquin. Which reminds me—"

He dialed. He got the acting captain in charge of the precinct squad at the West Fifty-fourth Street station. The precinct man had finished with Room 912 at the Algonquin. They had sealed it up after removing Miss Lacey's possessions and depositing them with the property clerk. Savings-account bankbooks? "Hold it, Nate. Got a list here."

Nathan held it.

"Yeah. Five of them. All in Mobile, Alabama. Total deposits of—hold it a minute."

Nathan held it.

"Eighty thousand seven hundred and twenty-three dollars and ninety-three—no, make that ninety-six—cents."

"Joint accounts, Captain? With her brother, say?"

"Just Jo-An Lacey. What the list says, anyway. Property clerk has the books now. Along with her clothes and what not."

Nathan Shapiro said, "Thanks, Captain," and hung up. He told Tony Cook what he had been told.

"Of course there may—" Shapiro said, and again the telephone interrupted him. He gave his name and listened. He said, "Did you get the number?" He said, "Good," and wrote down a number. He matched the license number with one in his mind. He said, "All right. Check in," and hung up.

"A black Cadillac showed up at the Algonquin," he told Tony Cook. "Chauffeur got out and went in. Came back in a couple of minutes with Lacey the Third. Drove away with him. Looks as if Lacey's going to have the weekend in the country."

Tony Cook waited.

"Because," Nathan said, "the car was Oscar Karn's. Thoughtful man, Karn. Offers a sympathetic hand to hold onto, probably."

"Or else," Tony said.

"As you say," Nathan said. "Mmmm."

"Comes to better than ninety grand," Tony said. "In ready cash. It must pay to write novels."

"I wouldn't know," Shapiro said. "She had a smash hit. With maybe another one coming up."

"And maybe," Tony said, "a safe-deposit box full of securities. In Mobile."

"Ninety thousand will do for a start," Nathan Shapiro said. "Oh, we'll check up through channels. Banks are stuffy about things like that, but we'll check up. These parties you've been to with Rachel. Down in the Village?"

"One or two of them. One uptown. Park Avenue."

"Painters, writers, composers? That sort of people? Rachel seems to get around. Editors, maybe?"

"They didn't wear labels," Tony said. "Yes, she knows a good many people. Gets invited around a good deal. Used to, anyway. Recently—" He broke it off there.

Nathan Shapiro merely nodded his head. Then he said, "She's intelligent as well as decorative, from what I've seen of her. Does she do any of these things herself? Paint? Write? That sort of thing?"

"Once she told me she 'dabbles,'" Tony said. "Didn't say at what. And I've never pressed her. What she wants to tell me she tells me. You getting at something, Nate?"

"Not about you and Rachel. Your business and hers. You're seeing her tomorrow night, Tony? Going to one of these parties, maybe?"

"I'd planned to take her to dinner. But, from what you said, I gather I'll be working. Day off or not."

"According to the schedule," Shapiro said, "it's your day off. We can stick to schedule. Pretty much, anyway. Just taking her to dinner? No party?"

"No party, Nate. Just—well, just—"

"Yes," Shapiro said. "Maybe she was invited to a party, you think? Tomorrow being a Saturday. And turned it down because she had a date with you? A party to which you could, as you put it, tag along? With your ears open?"

"Not that I know of. Of course, she wouldn't make a—"

He stopped. Nathan Shapiro finished for him. "Make a point

89

of having turned down a party to have dinner with you," he said. "I'm sure of that. From what little Rose and I have seen of Miss Farmer. There'll be a good deal of talk about Miss Lacey when people—people in her line of work especially— get together. She's been identified as Jo-An Lacey, you know. It's been on radio and television. The *News* is already on the street with it. The *Times* will be. There'll be a lot of talk about it, I'd think."

Tony said, "Well." He said it slowly. He said, "These people will be friends of hers, Nate. Acquaintances, anyway. You'd—I mean I'd—be—well, asking her to be my cover."

"She's a friend of yours too, Tony. I'm not suggesting you wear a disguise or anything like that. You'll be Detective Anthony Cook. I suppose you were at these other parties?"

"Sure. Only—"

"You'll just be keeping your ears open," Shapiro said. "For talk about the Karn outfit. About this Laurence Shepley. Who maybe knows some of the same people. Has he been at any of these parties you've been to?"

"No. Of course, people come in and out. Rachel and I—well, we usually've left early. She'd never seen Shepley until last night. When he was at the Charles bar. But, sure, he'd probably bump into other writers. Go, maybe, to the same parties."

Shapiro looked at his watch.

"It's not quite ten," he said. "Miss Farmer will still be awake?"

Tony didn't know. He said she'd expected to have a hard day. He said maybe she'd already have gone to sleep.

"I doubt whether she'd much mind your waking her up," Shapiro said. "Use the booth outside, huh?"

Tony sighed. His sigh wasn't up to any of Nathan Shapiro's, but it was a good enough sigh.

Rachel answered on the second ring. She did not sound particularly as if she had been wakened. She did say, "*What on earth, Tony?*"

He told her what on earth. She said, "Why on earth?" and Tony told her why. She said, "It sounds a little like spying, doesn't it?" and Tony said she could call it that and say no and that they'd have dinner together as they'd planned and that that would be, on the whole, a hell of a lot more fun.

"The Pierces are having a few people in for drinks," Rachel said. "They asked me to drop by if I was free and I said maybe, the way one does. From five-thirty on, Angela said. Angela Pierce and Tommy Pierce. You've met them. He's with one of the book publishers, as it happens."

"Little blonde with blue eyes? Good figure and doesn't mind showing it?"

"You remember the wrong Pierce," Rachel said. "It would be better if you remembered a tall, sort of gangly man with a neat black mustache. Which would be Tommy. But all right. Five-thirty will mean more like six-thirty, you know. And they're only a few blocks away."

"Six," Tony said. "When I'll be around, I mean."

"All right, Tony."

"Was it a hard day?"

"Enough to make my feet hurt. Good night, Tony."

"I'm very fond of your feet, Rachel."

"Good night, Anthony."

Tony went back to Nathan Shapiro's office. Shapiro was just hanging up the telephone.

"The State Police are keeping an eye on Karn's place," Shapiro said. "Just to see that Lacey gets there all right. No reason he shouldn't that I can see. Well?"

"All right," Tony said. "She's been asked to drop in for cocktails with some people called Pierce. They're having a few people in. She's not particularly enthusiastic, but—all right. And this man Pierce—seems I've met him but I don't remember much about him—seems he works for a book publisher."

"Well," Shapiro said, "sometimes we've got to get the breaks. Maybe this is one of the times."

He did not speak as if he expected it to be one of the times.

91

9

Tonight she was wearing a white sleeveless dress with a wide yellow belt. She even had it on when she opened the door for Tony Cook at six o'clock—at, actually, a few minutes before six. He put his arms around her, and for a moment he thought she resisted. Then she didn't. She said, "Oh, all right. But your gun bangs into me. Do you have to wear it tonight?"

"The regulations require," Tony said and looked at her and got the odd, indefinable impression that his required gun was, for that evening, a symbol. He said, "All right, to hell with the regulations. I could get busted, but—all right."

"Nobody will frisk you," Rachel told him, and then smiled her wide smile. "Sometimes," Rachel Farmer said, "I think I like you."

Tony took off the shoulder holster and the gun in it. He felt lighter without it and, in a fashion, bereft.

"They live on Thompson Street," Rachel said. "Down below the Square. You know those houses? A row on Thompson and a row on Sullivan, with a common garden between them for the whole block. The people who own the houses own the garden. They've even got statues in it. They've got private guards, of course. It's—oh, a kind of community. But all the houses are old houses."

They walked down to Waverly Place and cut across Washington Square to Thompson Street. It took them about ten minutes. A uniformed man from a private protection agency was walking toward them along Thompson when they got to it.

"They own the whole house," Rachel said. "There are apartments in some of the houses, but mostly they're just houses. Here we are."

She led the way up scrubbed white steps between polished brass handrails. Neither of them needed the help of the handrails. Tony pressed a button, and chimes sounded softly from within the Pierce house—a three-story house of white-painted brick.

Thomas Pierce was a tall, somewhat gangly man with a neat black mustache. Tony still remembered him only vaguely. He looked at Tony as if he did not remember him at all, but he beamed at Rachel. He said, "Good girl. Angie said you were afraid you couldn't make it."

"Things changed a little," Rachel said. "You remember Tony Cook, Tommy?"

"Sure," Tommy Pierce said, with great conviction in his voice. Tony suspected the conviction did not really belong there. Pierce grasped his hand firmly. He said, "Swell you could come along, Cook." Tony said it was good of them to let him barge in. They went in.

The long, not-wide room they went into had windows at the far end—ceiling-to-floor windows. There was a garden beyond them. There were half a dozen people in the room. They were clustered in a rough circle around a big coffee table. All of them had drinks.

"Probably know everybody," Pierce said, and the three men in the room stood up. "Angie," Pierce said, "Rache made it after all. And brought a friend with her to even things."

A slim blond woman, with a dress which clung to an admirable body, stood up. She said, "Rache, darling," and came across the room with both hands held out. Rachel Farmer took both the extended hands. She said, "This is Tony Cook, Angie. I think you and Tommy met him once at the Petersons'."

"Of course," Angela Pierce said, There was as much conviction in her voice as there had been in her husband's, but Tony thought it was more firmly based. "Wonderful of you to bring him, darling. Sherry, Rache? And you, Tony?"

First names were leaped on, snatched up, Tony Cook thought. He said, "Bourbon, if you don't mind, Mrs. Pierce."

Angela Pierce said, "Tommy?" and Thomas Pierce went down the room to a table under the windows. There were bottles on the table and glasses and a large ice bucket. Pierce began to rattle ice into a glass; to pour from a bottle.

"You all know Rache," Angela Pierce said. It appeared to Tony that everybody did. "And this is Tony Cook." They murmured pleasantly at Tony. They were all young or youngish, Tony thought. Only one of the men had aggressively long hair. He didn't know any of—

He stopped that thought in the middle of it. He did know one of the men, one of the politely standing men. For the moment he could not remember the man's name. The man, who was of medium height and a little older than the others—old enough for thick gray hair—came toward Tony with his hand out. Tony took the offered hand.

"Hi, Mr. Cook," the gray-haired man said. "Still on the force?"

"Yes," Tony said, and remembered the man's name and where they had met. The man's name was Alvin Carson, and they had met with Tony sitting in a witness chair and Carson walking up and down in front of him and turning from time to time toward a jury.

"Yes, Mr. Carson," Tony said. "I'm still a policeman. You gave me rather a going-over a few years back."

Carson had been the lawyer defending a man charged with murdering his mistress. Tony had been a detective (3rd gr.) then. He had been a witness for the People of the State of New York. Carson had given him the memorable going-over on cross-examination. Carson had also got his client off with a manslaughter conviction, which was less than the District Attorney, New York County, had expected.

"Just doing my job," Carson said, and let go of Tony's hand, which he had been clutching firmly. "The way you were doing yours, Mr. Cook. So you're still at it."

"Yes," Tony said. "Still at it, Mr. Carson. But—off duty at the moment."

He realized that all the others in the room, except Rachel, were looking at him. So far as he could tell, they were looking at him without animosity. A good many people, even among the law-abiding, look at policemen with uneasiness, even animus.

"Enter the law," Pierce said, coming down the room with a wineglass in one hand and a squat glass with ice tinkling in it in the other. The wine in Rachel's glass was, Tony noticed, almost as dark in color as the bourbon in his. Well, they were Rachel's friends, even if they did call her "Rache" and offer her sweet sherry.

Tony took the glass held out to him and said, "Thanks," and was told to find a place to sit down. He found a place to sit down. It was next to Angela Pierce. Carson pulled up a chair and gestured toward the one he had vacated. Rachel sat in it. She was on the other side of the round table from Tony. She sipped from her glass and put it down on the table. She did not look at Tony, although he was looking at her. She smiled at Angela Pierce. To Tommy Pierce she said, "Perfect, Tommy." If Tony had not known her well, he would have thought she meant it. I shouldn't have dragged her into this, Tony thought. We should have gone uptown some place and had dinner by ourselves.

"We were all talking about poor Miss Lacey," Angela Pierce said. "Such an awful thing to happen. Jo-An Lacey, Tony."

"Yes," Tony said. "It was an awful thing, Mrs. Pierce. Did you know Miss Lacey?"

"Met her once," Angela Pierce said. "Some big brawl or other. Pen, Tommy?"

Tony could feel his face going blank. It seemed an odd time to be asking for a pen. Pierce, who was circulating with a mixer of martinis, grinned at him. "She means P.E.N., Tony," Pierce said. "Poets, essayists and novelists. Comes out to the right initials. No, it wasn't, Angie. A party for her Oss Karn gave when *Snake Country* came out. Several years ago. You're right, though. It was really a brawl. One of those do's where you meet everybody four times. And the guest of honor maybe once. Hazards of the trade, from where I sit."

He poured martini into a glass held out for him.

Tony said, "Trade, Mr. Pierce?"

Pierce put the mixing glass down on the table, where it would be within reach of those who needed it. He came around the table and pulled a chair up near, but a little behind, Tony Cook's.

"Publishing," he said. "Publishing books, writing books. Agents. Trade. Racket. Sometimes even part of an art. Not often, but sometimes. I'm in it at one end. Jo-An Lacey was in it at another. She was—all right, she was one of the people who make it more than a business. Or racket or whatever. She was one in—oh, in a thousand. Maybe in ten thousand. Did she kill herself, Cook? First they said she did. Cut her wrists and died in a bath. Old Roman custom. But then the police seemed to get in on it as if there were more to it than just suicide. And why the hell should she kill herself? She was going places. As a matter of fact, she had got places."

Thomas Pierce had, Tony realized, a carrying voice. It was carrying to everybody in the room.

"The police are in on it," Tony said. "It—all right. It doesn't seem as open-and-shut as it did at first. But that's in the morning papers by now. No secret about it. You're in the publishing business, Rachel tells me."

"He's senior editor at the Jefferson Press," Angela said.

"Head of the Trade Books Department, actually," Pierce said. "You're a detective, Tony. You're working on the case?"

"I'm assigned to Homicide," Tony said. "We're all working on the case. Sure."

"And you can give us the lowdown?"

"There isn't any lowdown yet," Tony said. "All right, we think Miss Lacey was murdered. There are just bits and pieces."

It wasn't going as Nate had planned it. Partly, of course, because Alvin Carson had, in a sense, put the finger on him.

"From what's going around," Pierce said, "she was finishing a new book. I don't know why I put it that way. Oss certainly hasn't been making any secret of it."

"Oss?"

He could guess. There was no special reason for making it clear that he could guess.

"Oscar Karn," Pierce said. "Oscar Karn, Inc." He pronounced it "ink."

"That's what we understand," Tony said.

It wasn't going to be a matter, a simple matter, of picking up gossip. He might as well nudge it. In any event, they had "all been talking about poor Miss Lacey."

"The manuscript—I suppose the manuscript of this new book of hers—wasn't in the apartment she'd rented on Gay Street. Or in her hotel room," Tony said.

"Probably already turned it in to Karn," Pierce said. "He'd seen part of it. Hundred pages or so. Anyway, that's what he told us. Said he was damned sure she'd hit it again. Maybe even hit it harder. Of course, he was talking it up big, under the circumstances. On the other hand, he's quite an editor. He dug her up to start with. Played along with her."

"Under what circumstances, Mr. Pierce? Some special circumstances?"

Pierce looked across the table at Alvin Carson. The look was pointed; it was a look which sought an answer.

"It's not especially secret," Carson said. "Nothing much is in the trade. Mr. Karn and Jefferson Press have been considering a merger. We've—er—been in consultation with Mr. Karn's legal advisers. What Tommy means—I assume what he means—is that if Mr. Karn can bring along a new book, a new successful book, by Jo-An Lacey, his—" He paused and sipped from his drink.

"His position would be considerably strengthened," he said. "That's what you were getting at, Tommy?"

"Up to Ronald Anderson," Pierce said. "He's the president. I just work there. But, yes. I suppose that was what was more or less in my mind. Strengthen his position puts it about right."

"Does his position need strengthening?" Tony asked, and

again Pierce looked across the room at Carson. Carson drank from his glass. Then he looked at Tony Cook.

"Mr. Cook," he said, "are you here in an official capacity? Because you're one of those who are investigating Miss Lacey's death?"

"I'm here," Tony said, "because I had a date with Miss Farmer, Counselor. And because she felt it would be all right if we dropped in for a drink."

"Not because you knew Mr. Pierce is a senior editor of the Jefferson Press. And that the Press and Oscar Karn, Incorporated, are considering a merger? And that Miss Lacey was one of Karn's authors?"

"I didn't know Mr. Pierce was with the Jefferson Press," Tony said. "Rachel said something about his being an editor. She didn't say for whom. Did you, Rachel?"

Rachel's glass of almost-certainly sweet sherry was barely touched. She looked at Tony for a moment and shook her head. Then she said, "No, Tony. I just said Tommy was an editor. No. I said he worked for one of the book publishers. I didn't say which one. And you did make a reservation at the restaurant, didn't you?"

Tony looked at his watch. It still wasn't seven o'clock. She isn't happy about any of this, Tony thought. She's wishing I'd left my badge at home, along with my gun. But after he had looked at his watch he shook his head at Rachel. He said, "Time to finish our drinks." She looked at her almost-full wineglass. Then she tilted her head up and looked at the ceiling. That way, she's got a lovely profile, Tony thought. Damn Nate anyway.

"We had heard rumors about this merger," Tony said to Carson and to Pierce. "No details. I take it that Karn needs a potentially successful book to take with him?"

Carson appeared to think that over. Then he said, "A potential best seller is always an asset, Mr. Cook." He said it in a tone which implied no likelihood of amplification.

"All right," Pierce said. "If she'd finished it."

"Of course," Tony said. "And if she hadn't, it's no asset. That's clear enough."

Pierce said, "Sure." Then he said, "Of course it depends on how far she'd got with it. And how much of an outline she had ahead. If it was almost done and the outline was clear enough, Karn might have got somebody to finish it. Explaining in a foreword, probably. Not a usual thing to do, but it's happened."

"Another writer who could—make it sound as if Miss Lacey had written it?"

"Well," Pierce said, "not too much as if she hadn't. And as I said, there'd probably be a foreword. 'Miss Lacey had not quite finished this book at the time of her tragic death. The concluding pages were written, following her outline, by—oh, by So and So.'"

"Have you any idea who this So and So might be, Mr. Pierce?"

"No. Another of Karn's authors, at a guess. But it's all guesswork, isn't it? Probably she'd finished the book. Probably Oss has got it tucked away in a safe. Anyway, I don't see what it would have to do with Jo-An Lacey's death."

"Neither do I," Tony said. "We just grope around, Mr. Pierce."

Tony finished his drink. He said, "Maybe we had better be getting along, Rachel. We told Shepley we'd meet him around seven-thirty."

He looked at Rachel. There was no flicker of astonishment in her face. Good girl, Tony thought. Sweet sherry and now this thrown at her out of, certainly, the blue. She drank from her glass. She didn't even make a face. She said, "Maybe we'd better, Tony," and put her glass down. She had almost emptied it.

The man with longish hair—a very slight man with a good deal of hair—put his highball glass down on the table. He said, "Larry Shepley? Man with a red beard?"

"Yes," Tony said. "You know Shepley, Mr.—?"

"Parks," the long-haired man said. "Francis Parks." He spoke his name as if Tony should recognize it; as if he should say, "Not *the* Francis Parks." Tony did know a man named Parks—"Bulldog" Parks. He'd arrested Bulldog a few years back on a charge of assault with a deadly weapon. Bulldog was in jail; also he did look a little like a bulldog. One with a bad temper.

"Yes, I know Larry," Parks said. "We had him a couple of times as a visiting lecturer. Magazine article writing. That was a year or so back."

Tony, who had leaned forward as if to stand up, raised his eyebrows.

"N.Y.U.," Parks said. "I teach there."

"Frank's an associate professor," Angela Pierce said. "He's also a poet. A very fine poet."

"So I teach for a living," Parks said. "'The Art of Poetry.' Damned pretentious name for the course, but it's what they held out for."

"About Shepley?" Tony said.

"Known him for several years is all," Parks said. "Used to write short stories, sometimes for the slicks. Then the slicks more or less gave up fiction so he started to write articles. Lives down here somewhere. I run into him now and then. No mistaking that beard of his."

"When you've run into him," Tony said, "was it ever with Miss Lacey? I mean, was he ever with Miss Lacey?"

"I never saw Miss Lacey," Parks said. "Oh—seen pictures of her. But you can't go by pictures. Yes, he was with a girl a couple of times, as I remember it. Little thing. Brown hair, I think. Wore it long. Down to her shoulders, anyway. You see a lot like her, actually."

"Did she have a Southern accent?"

"Didn't speak to her," Parks said. "Just said 'Hi' to Larry and went along."

"You said a couple of times with this girl," Tony said. "The same girl both times?"

"I'd guess so. Look, Mr. Cook, it's not me who's the detective. The kind that never forgets a face."

"I'm not that kind either," Tony said. "Handicap in my line of work. Miss Lacey weighed a hundred and four pounds. She had brown hair to her shoulders. She had a good figure. We've

100

been told she dressed well. Answer the description of this girl you saw with Shepley?"

"Well enough. And of hundreds—thousands—of young women."

Tony had a copy of the photograph, the head-and-shoulders photograph, of Jo-An Lacey in his pocket. So did hundreds of other policemen. Tony showed the photograph to Francis Parks.

Parks said, "Jo-An Lacey?" and Tony said, "Yes, Mr. Parks."

"Maybe yes, maybe no," Parks said. "Look, I didn't stop and stare at her and Shepley. Not either time I saw them together, assuming it was the same girl both times."

Did Parks happen to remember where he had seen Shepley, possibly with Jo-An Lacey? Did he happen to remember when?

"Two-three weeks ago," Parks said. "I think it was in the Square. I had a late class and was walking through the Square and passed them. Way I remember it, anyway. The other time —maybe a couple of days later—they were walking up Sixth Avenue. Somewhere around Ninth Street, as I remember it. I was with a friend of mine and we didn't stop. I just said 'Hi' and we went along."

Tony stood up and Rachel also stood up. "No reason to rush," Pierce said. Rachel said, "We do have this date, don't we, Tony?" Tony nodded his head and said they did. He also said, again, that it was good of the Pierces to let him barge in, and Pierce said, "Any time," and went with them to the door, after Rachel had said, "Good night, all of you."

They were on the sidewalk and had begun to walk toward Washington Square when Alvin Carson caught up with them.

"I take it," Carson said, "that that was a fishing expedition, Mr. Cook? Catch anything?"

Tony said, "Fishing expedition, Mr. Carson?"

"I take it," Carson said, falling into step with them, "that you're assigned to the investigation of Miss Lacey's death. That you came along with Miss Farmer to fish."

Tony said, "Do you, Mr. Carson?"

"To fish without much bait," Carson said. "That's the way it seemed to me. I've heard you work with Nathan Shapiro, who's probably in charge of the investigation. Anyway, his name was mentioned in the story in the *News* this evening. The early edition. I happen to have run into Lieutenant Shapiro a few times."

Tony didn't say anything. They just walked along.

"I'm an officer of the court," Carson said. "Don't do much criminal work any more. My firm is counsel for the Jefferson Press. The publishers Karn wants to merge with."

"I gathered that," Tony said. "And that you were being cagy about it."

"Oscar Karn," Carson said, "has published a couple of books of poetry by Parks. And as counsel for the Jefferson Press I'm —er—required to keep things confidential. But I'm also an officer of the court, as I said. I'm obligated to help the authorities in any way I can. You seemed interested in the projected merger. And also in Mr. Shepley."

"I'm interested in anything which relates to Miss Lacey's murder," Tony said.

Carson did not answer immediately. They reached Washington Square and walked into it. It was still light; the Square still, relatively, was safe to walk through.

"As you say," Tony said, "you're an officer of the court, Mr. Carson. I'd appreciate anything you can tell me that might relate to Miss Lacey's murder."

"You made that clear enough," Carson said. "That you were on a fishing expedition back there. I can, without violating the confidential relationship of lawyer and client, tell you one thing you seemed to be interested in."

Lawyers are inclined to cover any point with verbiage, Tony thought. He said he would be glad to hear anything Mr. Carson felt free to tell him.

"Karn needs this merger," Carson said. "It's common gossip in the trade. He hasn't been doing as well lately as he used to do. A good many of his books have—well, fizzled out. And his backlist is weak. It was he who suggested the merger. For the terms he wants he—well, he needs a lot more."

"Like?"

102

"Like a potential best seller," Carson said. "A smash hit like —well, say, like Miss Lacey's *Snake Country.*"

"Or this new one of hers?"

"If it's as good as *Snake Country*. If he owns the rights and can bring the book with him. If it's as good as he seems to think it is."

"And if she finished it," Tony said. "Or—or almost finished it? As Mr. Pierce suggested?"

"Of course," Carson said. "You understand I'm not an editor, Mr. Cook. I'm a lawyer, subject to instructions. Any decision as to the potential value of Miss Lacey's new book would be made by Ronald Anderson. He's president of the Jefferson Press. And Tommy Pierce would have a say, naturally. If they like it enough, after they've read the manuscript, Karn's bargaining position would be—well, considerably improved, let's say. Have you turned up the manuscript, Mr. Cook?"

"I haven't seen it," Tony said. Detectives can be cagy too.

They had crossed the Square and had come to Washington Square North, which beyond the Square continues as Waverly Place. A cab with its top light on was going west. Carson held up a hand and the cab swerved to the curb.

"I'm going uptown," Carson said, reaching for the cab's door handle. "Drop you two anywhere?"

Tony said he guessed not.

Holding the door handle, Carson turned to them.

"By the way," he said, "this man Shepley you seemed interested in. He's one of Karn's authors, I believe. Or was for a couple of books, anyway. Nonfiction as I understand it. Not too successful, either of them, from what I hear."

He opened the door and got into the taxi. The cab driver slapped his flag down.

"Pleasant to have met you, Miss Farmer," Carson said through the open window as the cab pulled away from the curb. "And you too, Cook."

"All right, mister," Rachel said. She nowadays called him "mister" only when she was a little annoyed at him. "Was it worth the trouble? And that awful sherry? And what's all this about our meeting Shepley?"

103

"We're not," Cook said. "We never were. I'm sorry about the sherry. Whether it was worth the trouble I don't know. Did you ever hear of somebody finishing somebody else's book?"

"I've heard of it happening," Rachel said. "Do we get some dinner now?"

"We might stop by and pick up my gun first," Tony said. "Where would you like to go, dear?"

"I," Rachel said, "would like to go to the Algonquin. If it isn't too late. Do you have to have a gun to have dinner at the Algonquin?"

"I," Tony Cook said, "am supposed to have a gun to go any place."

So they went across Sixth Avenue and into Gay Street and her apartment, and Tony put his gun on. And Rachel had a La Ina to take the taste of the sweet sherry out of her mouth, and Tony had a short bourbon. And they decided it was perhaps a little late to go uptown for dinner and walked the few blocks to André's and had dinner in the garden.

Tony half expected Laurence Shepley would be there, but he wasn't.

10

The Shapiros breakfast late on Sunday morning when Sunday happens to be Nathan's day off. They were breakfasting at a little after nine-thirty, and sunlight was coming through the windows of their Brooklyn apartment. Nathan was on his third cup of coffee and his second cigarette.

"It looks like being another nice day," Rose said, and lighted her first cigarette. Then she said, "You know it won't do you any good, dog," to Cleo, who was sitting and looking up, watching each bite her people took. She had been looking hopeful. When cigarettes were lighted she made a low, disappointed sound.

"You know you're never fed at table," Rose told Cleo. "Go eat your own breakfast."

Cleo, who declines to know that she is not fed at table, gave a low, disconsolate woof.

"It would be a nice day to do something," Rose said. "After we read the *Times*. Go for a walk or something."

Nathan said, "Mmmm." He added that after one had read the Sunday New York *Times* there is no day left to walk in. He stubbed out his cigarette and reached out toward the pack on the table in front of him. "No," Rose said. "You're supposed to count."

Nathan pulled back the hand which was hovering over the pack of cigarettes.

"And," Rose said, "I'm here, Nathan. If you haven't noticed it, I'm here."

"I know," Nathan Shapiro said. "I was just—just going over things."

"You always are," Rose said. "Always going over who killed somebody."

She got up and began to put dishes on a tray. She had lifted the tray when the telephone rang. She put the tray back down again. She said, "Damn! It's Sunday. You're off this Sunday." She crossed the room to the telephone and said, "Hullo?" to it. She said, "All right, Tony. He is," and Nathan Shapiro crossed the room and took the telephone from his wife. Rose said, "Damn!" again, and with somewhat more emphasis than before, and went back and picked up the tray.

"On Sunday morning?" Nathan said, with sad incredulity in his voice. He listened. He said, "All right. I'll meet you there. Did you—no, skip it. Tell me at the office."

He put the receiver in its cradle. Rose had come out of the kitchen and stood looking up at him. Then, slowly, she shook her head.

"I gather," Rose Shapiro said, "that I'll be the one to walk Cleo. By myself."

"I'm afraid so, darling," Nathan said. "A man walked into his office about eight o'clock this morning and got slugged by somebody who was already there."

"The precinct," Rose said, who had been married to a policeman for some years, "or Safe and Loft? Or was he killed?"

"Just knocked out," Shapiro told her, from the bedroom where he was dressing. "Only, he's a man Tony and I talked to yesterday. An authors' agent, he's called."

He came out of the bedroom, strapping on his shoulder holster.

"And again damn," Rose said. "And I thought it was going to be such a nice day."

"Maybe this afternoon," Nathan said and leaned down to kiss her. "Meanwhile, there's always the *Times*."

Rose pulled herself away. Then, gently, she slapped her husband's sad face.

"I should have married a certified public accountant," Rose Shapiro said. "A nine-to-fiver."

"Did you have one in mind?"

Shapiro put on a jacket to cover his gun. He tightened his necktie.

"No, dear," Rose said. "I never had one in mind. All I ever had in mind was a tall, thin policeman who came around to ask if the car parked in front of a fire hydrant was mine. And whom I told that I didn't have a car and never parked it in front of fire hydrants. Go on, dear, and find out why a man would be going into his office at eight o'clock on a Sunday morning."

Nathan went along. There were not many people on the street. Here and there was a woman wearing a hat, and sometimes a man with her dressed up for Sunday. Catholics returning from Mass, Nathan supposed, considering the hats the women were wearing. One of the women said, "Good morning, Mr. Shapiro," and he said, "Oh, good morning, Mrs. O'Hara," and thought there was abstraction in his voice. He said, "It's a fine morning," to make up for the abstraction and went down a flight of stairs to a subway platform. There was only one other man on the platform, and he was drunk. It was ten minutes before a train came along, and Nathan saw that the drunk got on it without falling between the cars. Which ended his responsibility for an early-morning drunk.

It was beginning to grow hazy in Manhattan as Shapiro walked from the subway station to the station house. It was going to be warmer than it had been the day before. It was going to be muggier.

He climbed the stairs to Homicide, Manhattan South. Tony Cook was already there, sitting at his desk. Phillips Morton was sitting beside the desk. Morton had one hand covering the left side of his jaw. Holding a hand against a bruised jaw doesn't help the jaw any, but one always thinks it may.

"Morning, Tony," Nathan said. "Good morning, Mr. Morton. Had a spot of trouble, I hear."

"You're damned right," Morton said and took his hand away from his jaw. The jaw was swelling, and there was an adhesive bandage on it.

Shapiro said they had better go along to his office, and they went along to his office. Shapiro sat at his desk and Tony and Phillips Morton sat on the other two chairs.

"Mr. Morton just got here," Tony said. "Called the precinct when he came to and then, thinking it was a hell of a funny coincidence, called in here. And Lenny Johnson, who was catching, suggested he call me."

"And you called me," Shapiro said. "All right, Mr. Morton, you've probably been over it, but you'll want to go over it again. What happened?"

"Sometimes I go to my office early Sundays," Morton said. "Catch up on things. And read manuscripts. Telephone doesn't keep ringing the way it does at the apartment. Writers—some of them—want agents to do the damnedest things. Buy flowers for their girls' birthdays. You wouldn't believe it, Lieutenant."

"This morning?" Shapiro said.

Morton had got to his office about eight o'clock. He had signed in in the lobby, as was the regulation—recently the regulation. "There's a company doing Government work on one of the floors. And there's some sort of an Egyptian agency on another." He had unlocked his office door. Yes, so far as he could tell, the door was locked. Anyway, he had used his key.

"And this guy—a big guy—came charging out of the inside office and slugged me."

"With a weapon?"

"With his fist, far's I could tell. Anyway, he knocked me out. I was out—oh, maybe ten-fifteen minutes. I was still groggy when I looked at my watch."

"Did you get a good look at this man who hit you, Mr. Morton?"

"I suppose so. Sure, I must have. Only—well, he came out of nowhere. A big man. In a dark suit, I think. But—it was all so damn sudden. And unexpected. Here I go to my own office, where it'll be quiet, to read a manuscript and somebody busts out of my office and slugs me. It was all—it was all too sudden,

108

I guess. Too sudden to take in until it was—well, until it was over."

"Yes," Shapiro said. "Things are, sometimes. Was there money in your office, Mr. Morton? A safe or anything like that?"

"No. Checks made out to me as agent for writers. No money. Oh, I had about a hundred dollars in my wallet. I've still got it."

"You called the police when you came to," Shapiro said. "Who came?"

"Two men in uniform. Very quickly. Then two men not in uniform, who asked a lot of questions."

"Safe and Loft Squad," Tony said. "I checked. They figure the lock was picked. By a pro. Seven people had signed into the building. All legitimate. But there's only one man on duty in the lobby. Automatic elevators, of course. It wouldn't have been too hard."

"Apparently it wasn't," Shapiro said. "They didn't take your wallet, Mr. Morton. There wasn't any cash in your office. Not money, evidently. What was this man after?"

"File folders," Morton said. "From the temporary files; the permanent files are in locked cases. The folders, Lieutenant, from L through S. Letters from writers. Mostly about shaking money out of publishers. That sort of thing. Letters telling me that So and So gets a seventy-thirty break on subsidiaries and why doesn't he? Stuff that I'll get around to answering."

"And," Shapiro said, "your correspondence with Jo-An Lacey? Say, a letter telling you she wanted you as her agent?"

"No. Just the contract she was going to sign tomorrow when she brought in the rest of the manuscript. Which hasn't any value since nobody's signed it. The publishers hadn't. She hadn't. Oh, and a letter—one of those confirming-our-telephone-conversation sort of things. Not specifying the conversation, as I remember. That was all. She'd just come to me. I told you that. Had been going to come to me."

"Yes," Shapiro said. "Did you tell anybody you had this contract ready and that she hadn't signed it?"

"No. I don't shoot my mouth off about people in my stable, Lieutenant."

"But she may have told somebody."

"Sure."

"And somebody may have assumed she had already signed this contract?"

Morton supposed it was possible. He had no way of knowing.

"Neither have we," Shapiro said. "Yes, Tony?"

Tony Cook had not said anything. He had not moved. It must, Tony thought, have been something in his face, although he had not been conscious that Shapiro had been looking at him.

"When Miss Lacey said she was bringing around the manuscript of this new book," Tony said, "you gathered it was a finished manuscript? Or did she say it would be?"

"She said something like she was pretty sure she'd have it all wrapped up by Monday. Some writers keep diddling around with things they've written. Don't like to let go of them."

"Was she one of those?"

"I wouldn't know," Morton said.

"When she gave you the carbons of these first few chapters of 'Lonely Waters,'" Tony said, "did she give you an outline of the rest of it? Something to show the publishers?"

"No. It was my understanding that she had completed a first draft, but was making some changes. Finishing, mainly, would mean revising the rest of the book in line with earlier changes. And polishing, of course."

"Did you ever hear of some other writer's finishing a book when the original writer died before it was finished?"

"It's happened," Morton said. "Mostly when there are two people collaborating on a book, of course. The one who doesn't die finishes it. But sometimes a publisher who gets hold of a not-quite-finished book he's hot for may get another writer to finish it. It's never happened to any of my people, but I've heard of it. Nothing wrong with it, is there?"

"I wouldn't see anything," Nathan Shapiro said. "The publisher would explain, I suppose?"

110

"Sure," Morton said. "I'd think so. As I said, I've no firsthand experience with that sort of thing."

"L through S," Shapiro said. "Laurence Shepley a client of yours, Mr. Morton? I gather he recommended you to Miss Lacey."

"Yes," Morton said. "Larry's a client of mine. I've sold some pieces of his. A couple of them expanded into books."

"The books," Tony said. "Did the Karn people publish them?"

"Yes. Come to think of it, yes."

"Were they successful books, Mr. Morton?"

Morton started to rub his bruised jaw. He thought better of it. He said, "Ouch!" Then he said, "Moderately. What I mean is, they paid their way. Just about. Production costs keep on going up. At a guess, Oss Karn didn't lose on them. Didn't make much, either."

"And Shepley himself?"

Morton said, "Huh?" He said, "Sorry. My jaw hurts."

"We won't keep you much longer," Shapiro said. "What Detective Cook is wondering, did Mr. Shepley make much from these books?"

"He didn't get rich from them," Morton said. "Thing is, he's not getting rich from much of anything nowadays. Did better when there was a fiction market. Short fiction, I mean. Between us, he's just about getting by."

"Which cuts your commissions, of course."

"Sure."

Again, Nathan Shapiro said, "Yes, Tony?" although Tony Cook hadn't said anything.

"If, say, Karn wanted somebody to finish Miss Lacey's book," Tony said. "We don't know it needed finishing, of course. Suppose it did. Would you think he might ask Shepley to do it?"

Morton shrugged his shoulders. He winced slightly. It hurts to shrug shoulders under a badly bruised jaw.

"Well," he said, "Larry used to write fiction. Not long stuff. Not novel-lengths. But he's a pro. Come to think of it, he was originally from down South somewhere. As Miss Lacey was.

111

But hell, I'm pretty sure Jo-An had finished the book. And she was going to bring the manuscript in to me tomorrow."

"Apparently," Shapiro said, "she sent it in to Karn instead. At least, he says it showed up at his office. In the mail."

"All of it, Lieutenant?"

"I don't know," Shapiro said. "He hadn't seen it himself when I talked to him. Anyway, he said he hadn't. We'll have a look at it tomorrow. Meanwhile—assume it was not finished. Assume Shepley had been asked to finish it. Would such an arrangement have been cleared through you, Mr. Morton?" Shapiro shook his head sadly. "I don't understand how these things are handled, you see."

"Maybe yes, maybe no," Morton said. "If he thought I could get him a better deal, Larry'd probably have come to me. If he was satisfied, no reason he should. I haven't an over-all contract with him. Not with any of my people. I told you that, didn't I?"

"Yes," Shapiro said. "Just an agency clause in book contracts. Shepley hadn't taken it up with you? If, of course, there was anything to take up?"

"No."

"So there wouldn't be anything in his file folder relating to that? Any correspondence of any kind?"

"No. As a matter of fact, I don't think there was much of anything in Larry's folder. Wait a minute. As I remember, a magazine contract for something of his. My copy of it. The check had come through and I'd sent mine to him. It would have gone into the permanent files any time. Any time I'm not between secretaries. Only most of the time I am between secretaries, damn it. Kids come in and louse things up for a couple of weeks and quit. Or I fire them. Kids who want to be writers and think working for an agent is a way in, the poor innocents."

"By the way," Tony said, "do you know a man named Parks, Mr. Morton? Francis Parks? He's a poet, as I understand it. Karn has brought out a book or two of his."

"Of him," Morton said. "They say he's an all-right poet. Not one of my people. I don't handle poets. I've got enough trouble without poets. I don't know who's published Parks. In book form, that is. He's had a few things in *The New Yorker*. Nothing I could make anything out of, but I'm a Yeats type, myself. Why'd you ask about Parks, Mr. Cook?"

"Just somebody I ran into at a party the other night," Tony said. "Knows Shepley slightly. Has seen him around in the Village with a girl who could have been Miss Lacey. But we already knew Shepley was seeing Miss Lacey. Seems Shepley's given occasional lectures at N.Y.U. About magazine article writing, according to Mr. Parks. Make arrangements for that sort of thing through you, Mr. Morton?"

"No. Not my line of country. Lecture agent, possibly. Direct contact, more likely. I didn't know he'd been giving lectures. But—I guess anything that would make him a buck. An honest buck. Larry's an honest guy."

"I'm sure he is," Shapiro said. "You can't tell us anything more about this man who attacked you, Mr. Morton?"

"I told you I can't," Morton said. "Just—oh, just a sudden movement. Then I came to on the floor."

"I see," Shapiro said. "It happens that way a lot of times. Just a sudden movement and—was this sudden movement wearing a beard, Mr. Morton?"

"I keep on telling you I—" Morton said, and then stopped and looked hard across Shapiro's desk. "If you're thinking of Larry Shepley, forget it," Morton said. "Larry's a friend of mine."

"All right," Nathan Shapiro said. "We can't really forget anybody, but all right. I gather your face got cut when this man hit you. Badly?"

Morton put a hand up to his damaged jaw. He touched the adhesive bandage.

"Just a nick," Morton said. "Bled a little. Isn't bleeding now. Just a nick. He had hard knuckles, I suppose."

"Or was wearing a ring," Shapiro said. "Left side of your jaw. Hit you with his right hand? Or don't you remember?"

"As far as I know," Morton said, "he could have hit me with a baseball bat."

"Go home and put an ice bag on it," Shapiro said. "If we

113

need to—and probably we will need to—we'll get in touch."

They let Phillips Morton find his own way out.

"It's all very confusing," Shapiro said. "All of this is confusing. If Miss Lacey hadn't signed this contract and the publishers hadn't, why steal it? Who were the publishers, by the way? My memory's going."

"Materson and Brothers," Tony said. "So's mine."

"For one thing," Shapiro said, "there are too many publishers mixed up in this. Along with too many beards."

"If somebody didn't know it wasn't signed," Tony said.

"Anybody could have looked," Nathan Shapiro said. "Of course, they didn't know Morton was going to barge in. Speaking of barging in, how did the party you and Miss Farmer went to go?"

Tony told him how the party had gone, which was not precisely as they had hoped it would go. When Tony had finished, Nathan Shapiro nodded his head sadly. "Of course," he said, "this man Carson's not a disinterested party. Works for this Jefferson Press. Represents them, anyway. To their advantage to play down the value of Karn, Incorporated. We'll have to ask around. Any idea who we might ask?"

Tony didn't have.

"Anyway," Shapiro said, "it's Sunday and it's summer. There'll be nobody around to ask. Except—I think we'd better go and talk with Mr. Shepley, don't you?"

"It's Sunday for him too," Tony said. "It's summer for him too. He's probably got a telephone. I could give him a ring."

"No," Shapiro said. "We'll just drop in, I think."

They went in an unmarked police car down to West Twelfth Street. Tony pressed the button over the slip with "Laurence Shepley" typed on it. They waited for the door release to click. It did not. Tony put his thumb hard on the button and kept it there for some seconds. Nothing came of that, either. "Well," Tony said, "I live here too." He got his key out. They climbed a flight of stairs. "Where I live," Tony said, indicating a door. They climbed on. "Where he lives," Tony said, stopping in front of a door on the fourth floor.

"When he's home," Shapiro said, and knocked on the door.

114

He knocked hard on the door, and at first nothing came of it. Then there was a muffled voice from beyond the door. The words were not clear, but there seemed to be anger in the voice. The voice sounded like that of a man swearing. More or less involuntarily, Nathan Shapiro and Anthony Cook moved to opposite sides of the door. Trained policemen have involuntary reactions. This sometimes keeps them alive.

When Laurence Shepley yanked the door open, he looked angry, but not threatening. He had nothing to threaten with. He was wearing a terry-cloth robe which was a little too short for him and his red beard was ruffled. He glared at them. He said, "Now what the hell?"

"Just a question or two, Mr. Shepley," Shapiro said. "Can we come in?"

"You sure as hell can't," Shepley said. "Unless you've got a warrant or something. Damn it all, it's Sunday, and it's the crack of dawn."

"It's almost noon," Shapiro said. "No, we haven't got a warrant of any kind, Mr. Shepley."

"Dawn cracks late on Sunday," Shepley said. "What do you want? If it's about Jo-An Lacey, I've told you all there is to tell. I knew her casually. Took her to dinner a couple of times."

He said the last sentence in a loud voice, like one who wants to be overheard.

"Anyway," Shepley said, "I've got a friend with me. You waked us both up. And he—"

"Who is it, Larry?"

It was not a man inside the apartment who wanted to know who had roused them at this ungodly hour of a Sunday. Nathan hadn't supposed it would be.

"Damn it to hell," Shepley said, raising his voice again. "A couple of cops. Want to ask me questions."

"Dear Larry," the woman—a young woman from her voice —said. "I hope you have the answers, dear."

Shepley came out and closed the door after him. He said, "All right. It any of your business?"

"None," Shapiro said. "Suppose you get dressed, Mr. Shepley, and come down to Mr. Cook's apartment. That way we won't have to go on disturbing your friend."

Shepley continued to glare. He did start to smooth his beard down with both hands.

"No compulsion," Shapiro said. "Just as—well, call it a favor. And cooperation with the police. We won't keep you long."

Shepley said "Damn it to hell" again. But the violence had somehow leaked out of his voice. He said, "Oh, all right. I'll come down."

He went back into his apartment and closed the door after him. He did not slam the door.

They waited in Tony's apartment with the door to the stairs open. "Anyway," Tony said, "we won't have to wait for him to shave." It was five minutes or so before they heard feet coming down the stairs. Shepley had put his shoes on. And Tony had boiling water almost finished dripping through the coffee in the Chemex.

Shepley was wearing slacks and a white polo shirt. His beard was neat again. He said, "All right. I'm sorry I yelled at you," and said that, yes, he could do with some coffee.

"We're sorry to break in on you," Shapiro said. "I'm afraid we picked a bad time."

"You sure as hell did," Shepley said and that he'd take his coffee black.

Tony poured coffee into three cups. He added cream to his and a lump of sugar to Nathan's.

"If it's more about the Lacey girl," Shepley said, "there isn't any more. I ran into her at a party and saw her a few times afterwards. I didn't sleep with her or particularly want to. I've got a—I think I told you—a regular girl. The one upstairs. Not that Jo-An wasn't a sweet, pretty kid for all she was one hell of a novelist, but all we did was to have dinner a couple of times and talk."

"I don't question that," Shapiro said. "I hope your—regular girl won't."

"Well," Shepley said, "I can't say you're doing me any good. But I'll make out. What are these questions that are so damned important?"

116

"When you were talking with Miss Lacey," Shapiro said, "did you talk about this new book of hers? The one she was working on when she died?"

"Not much," Shepley said. "She wasn't the kind who talk their books. Oh, they're around, but she wasn't one of them."

"Did you gather she'd finished the book?"

"Or thereabouts," Shepley said. "Oh, I gathered she had a bit more to do on it. Things in it she thought she could perhaps make better. That's an occupational complaint, Lieutenant. Some of us have it worse than others."

"But you gathered she was about finished? About ready to turn it in to her publisher?"

"She brought it up here from the South," Shepley said. "Sure, it must have been finished, or damn near finished."

"But she rented this apartment in Gay Street so that she could do more work on it?"

"I guess so. I was never in this Gay Street place of hers. I told you that, didn't I?"

"Yes. You were from the South yourself, originally, Mr. Shepley?"

"My God," Shepley said. "Can you still hear it? Yes. Georgia. I didn't know I still sounded like it."

"You don't," Shapiro said. "Not to me anyway. A man said something about it, is all. A man named Morton. Your agent, isn't he?"

"Yes. And a damned nice guy. Does it make any difference I was born in Georgia, Lieutenant? Lots of people are."

"It doesn't make any difference where you were born," Shapiro said. "You and Miss Lacey were both from the South. Brought you together somewhat, perhaps."

"My God," Shepley said. "We're not a pack, Lieutenant. Some of my best enemies are Southerners." He looked at Shapiro's sad face. He said, "Sorry I put it exactly that way."

Shapiro said, "Enemies, Mr. Shepley?"

"Just a paraphrase," Shepley said. "A damned stupid one. I don't have any special enemies I know of."

"About Mr. Morton," Shapiro said, "he handles all your work for you?"

117

"Not all of it. Most of it."

"And you sold, through him, a couple of books to this Oscar Karn concern?"

"Yes."

"You think Miss Lacey had finished her book," Shapiro said. "Or almost finished it. There wasn't—hasn't been since she died—any question of your finishing it?"

Shepley said he didn't get it.

"We've heard it sometimes happens," Shapiro said. "An author dies with a manuscript not quite completed. The publisher gets somebody else—somebody in whom he has confidence, I suppose—to finish it."

Shepley shrugged his shoulders. He had strong shoulders, Shapiro noted. He said, "Maybe it happens," in a doubtful voice. "Can't say I've ever heard of its happening. And nobody in his right mind would ask me to finish a book by Jo-An Lacey. For one thing, I don't write at all the way she wrote. If her book wasn't finished, and some publisher wanted a writer to finish it, he'd get another woman. Unless he was a damn fool."

"If you had agreed to finish somebody else's book," Shapiro said, "Mr. Morton would have handled the arrangements?"

"Probably. But I didn't. Nobody asked me to. Anyway, I've got my own work."

Shapiro said, "Of course." He said, "Mr. Morton had an unpleasant experience this morning. A rather baffling experience."

He told Shepley about Morton's experience.

Shepley said, "Jesus! Was he banged up badly?"

"He'll live," Shapiro said.

"Just the files? L to S? Wait a minute. That would take in Lacey to Shepley."

"Yes," Shapiro said. "A contract Morton had arranged between Miss Lacey and a publisher. Not Oscar Karn, Incorporated. A contract which hadn't been signed by her or the publisher."

Shepley said he didn't get it. Shapiro said, "We don't, either,

118

Mr. Shepley. Would there have been anything special in your file, Mr. Shepley?"

Not that Shepley knew of. Then he laughed.

"Maybe Xeroxes of letters from magazine editors," Shepley said. "Saying, 'Thanks for letting us see this very interesting article by Laurence Shepley. We're sorry the consensus is that it's not for us.' Only I don't know that Phil has them copied. Can't think of any reason why he should. Nothing much else I can think of. I send pieces in to Phil and he sells them or he doesn't sell them. Doesn't require much correspondence."

Shapiro nodded his head.

"Then if that's all you want—" Shepley said and finished his coffee and started to stand up.

There was the click of a woman's heels on the staircase outside Cook's apartment. The clicking sound receded down the stairs.

"Damn," Shepley said. "I guess there's no great hurry now. So if you want to go on with your grilling, Lieutenant?"

"Not grilling," Shapiro said. "Just a search for information. There is one more thing you might be able to help us with."

"If I can. Sure."

"During the time you knew Miss Lacey," Shapiro said, "did you and she run into other people she knew? Other friends of hers?"

"I suppose so. Sure, one or two. And people did recognize her. Say things like, 'Aren't you Jo-An Lacey? I've heard so much about you. And I just love your books.' Crap like that. Probably happened to her all the time."

"Probably," Shapiro said. "You didn't run into any close friends of hers, I take it?"

"No. Not that I recall, anyway."

"Did she mention any close friends? Here in New York, I mean?"

"Look," Shepley said. "I keep telling you we just had a—oh, a damn casual acquaintance. I took her to dinner a couple of times. We had drinks a couple of times and talked about our trade. That was the size of it."

Nathan Shapiro said he saw. He said, "People get impres-

119

sions, Mr. Shepley. I'm sure you did about Miss Lacey. One of them, say, whether she had, here in New York, any—call it close relationship with anybody. Did you?"

"I had a feeling she was pretty much on her own. More or less a loner, actually. Up here, anyway. Of course—" He broke off. He looked at the coffee cup he'd just emptied. Tony Cook got up and refilled it.

Shepley said, "Thanks." Then he said, "Of course, sometimes when I called her up for a date—just a date for drinks or dinner—she'd be tied up. Or say she was. But everybody's tied up sometimes."

"Of course," Shapiro said. "She didn't give you any idea how she was tied up? Who with, I mean?"

"No. Why the hell should she?"

"No reason," Shapiro said. "You see, Mr. Shepley, whoever killed her obviously knew about this Gay Street place of hers. May have gone to see her there several times. We don't know, of course. We—well, we just have to ask around."

"All I know about her is what I've told you," Shepley said. "Took her to dinner a couple of times. Met her at the Algonquin. Had drinks with her a couple of times. Once in the Algonquin lobby. Once she came to my apartment upstairs and we had a drink or two and talked a lot. Nothing that would interest the morals squad of yours. I keep telling you that."

"I know you do," Shapiro said. "And we don't keep asking. You met her a few times, as writer to writer. I don't doubt you, Mr. Shepley. So that's all you can tell us about her personal life?"

"Yes."

"And you were never at her apartment?"

Shepley sighed heavily—a sigh of boredom. He said, "No," at the end of the sigh and said it wearily.

"When you made engagements with her you did it by telephone? Called her at the Algonquin?"

"Usually. She did give me a number to call if she wasn't at the hotel. Said something about its being a hideout to work in. I called that once or twice and—"

He stopped abruptly. He said, "Has either of you got a cigarette? I left mine upstairs."

Tony gave him a cigarette and a light for it. Shepley drew heavily on the cigarette.

"I just thought of something," Shepley said. "Not that it means anything, probably. Once when I called this hideaway number a man answered. I asked if Miss Lacey was there and he said something like, 'No Miss Lacey here. Afraid you've got the wrong number,' and I said, 'Sorry,' and hung up. I figured I'd dialed wrong, and after a bit I had another try at it. Got Jo-An that time, all right. But it was one of the times she was tied up."

"It's easy enough to make a mistake when dialing," Shapiro said.

Shepley said, "Sure." Then he said, "Can't say I do very often. Must have that time, obviously."

"This man who answered. You didn't recognize his voice?"

"No, Lieutenant, I didn't recognize his voice." He stubbed out his half finished cigarette and said, "Anything else, Lieutenant?"

"I don't think so," Shapiro said. "Sorry we had to break in on you at a bad time. I hope your friend wasn't too—"

"Oh," Shepley said, "she'll be back. And I'm sorry I yelled at you at first."

They watched Laurence Shepley go out of Cook's apartment. He didn't seem in much of a hurry.

11

In Shapiro's small, and increasingly hot, office they agreed that they came up with questions, not answers—particularly not with the big answer. They had a fact—somebody had put Nembutal in Jo-An Lacey's coffee and, when it had taken effect, had cut her wrists and put her in a bathtub to die. Drunk coffee with her and washed one of the cups and not the other? Why not the other?

"To make it look like suicide," Tony suggested and got "Mmmm" for an answer. Shapiro was flipping through papers he had taken out of his In basket.

The State Police reported that John Henry Lacey III—or a man answering his description—had been brought to Oscar Karn's house near Mount Kisco the night before and had been brought in Karn's Cadillac, driven by Kenneth Stokes, half of the couple who took care of the Karn house and of the Karns. State troopers get to know the people of their territory. Lacey apparently had spent the night with the Karns. At least, when a police cruiser had happened to be in the vicinity that morning—time 10:17—the Cadillac, still driven by Stokes, had come down the driveway with Oscar Karn and the subject in the back seat. The cruiser had happened to be going in the same direction as the Cadillac, and behind it. The Cadillac had gone to a country club, and when it was parked there, Stokes had taken golf clubs out of the trunk. Two sets of clubs. Karn, who was dressed for golf, and the presumptive Lacey, who was not, had waited their turn and teed off.

So—Karn was a considerate host and John Henry Lacey III was a golfer.

Shapiro lighted a cigarette. He said, "Yes, Tony, to make it look like suicide. Did Shepley make a mistake in dialing? Or was there really a man in the girl's apartment? Or is Shepley just feeding us a story?"

"And," Tony Cook said, "why would anybody want to steal an unsigned contract from an agent's office? If, of course, Morton didn't just walk into a door and bang his own jaw, to make things come out even. And—"

He stopped because Nathan Shapiro was looking at the ceiling. Involuntarily, Tony looked at the ceiling too. There was a fly walking on it. The fly didn't seem to be going any place in particular. Tony felt a measure of kinship with the fly.

"It's too bad most people don't keep diaries any more," Shapiro said. "At least I suppose the girl—"

He did not finish. Instead he reached for the telephone. He had to wait for a couple of minutes. He said, "Lieutenant Shapiro, Homicide South. Sergeant O'Rourke happen to be around?"

"Day off, Lieutenant. Sergeant Proskowitz speaking. Something I can do?"

"Effects of Miss Jo-An Lacey," Shapiro said. "Got a list handy, Sergeant?"

"Take a minute," Proskowitz said. "Yeah. Something special you want?"

"They include a desk calendar? Memo pad sort of thing? Or a diary?"

"Hold it," Proskowitz said and, almost at once, "Yeah. Calendar pad we've got. No diary."

Yes, he would send it up. And the lieutenant knew, of course, he would have to have a receipt.

"Yes," Shapiro said. "Send it along, Sergeant."

He hung up. He said, "I suppose we might have something to eat while we're waiting, Tony. If the place is open."

"It will be," Tony said. "Cops have got to eat."

In the squad room, they stopped by Lenny Johnson's desk and waited until he finished taking down a squeal. There would be a package coming from the property clerk. A signature on a receipt would be needed. Lenny, who was a new third-grade detective, said, "Sir."

Joe's Place was open. It was one o'clock on Sunday afternoon, and the bar was open. "Joe," whose name was Thomas, had to be careful about the law. Most of his customers were policemen. There were only men in Joe's Place when Shapiro and Tony Cook went into it. Two of the men were in uniform; the rest in civilian clothes. There were slight bulges in their jackets on the left side of their chests, except for one man who had the bulge on the right side. Detectives can be left-handed like anybody else.

Tony had the pot roast and a beer. Nathan had corn beef on rye and, since it was technically his day off, a glass of sherry to precede it. He could be sure of the sherry at Joe's Place. It wouldn't be that sharp stuff they called "dry." Nathan had iced coffee after his sandwich and Tony had another beer. They crossed the street and walked two blocks on the shady side and agreed that it was getting muggy as hell—too damned muggy for late June. July didn't bear thinking about in advance.

The office of the property clerk had been prompt. Lenny Johnson handed Shapiro a small, flat package and said, "Sir." They took the package into Shapiro's office, which was even hotter than it had been before lunch, and Nathan Shapiro opened the single window, which didn't help matters appreciably.

Jo-An's memo pad was small. It was open at Thursday, June 22. It was held open by a rubber band. There was no notation on the sheet for June 22. The last sheet she had turned over, Shapiro thought. If she had written a memo on it, what would the memo have been? "I die today?" Only she had, probably, died the twenty-first. After she had turned the sheet to a tomorrow which had never come.

The sheet for the twenty-first, when Nathan flicked back to

it, was as blank as that of the twenty-second. That was mildly disappointing. She had had a date that day, or that night. The time of death can only approximately be set even by the best of pathologists. Dead on the morning of Friday, the twenty-third. Dead then thirty-six hours or longer. It might have taken her some time to die in the bathtub. The water in which she had died might have been hot when she was put into it, which would somewhat obscure matters. Say the night of Wednesday, June 21. If she had had a date, she had not noted it on the calendar pad.

"We may as well start at the beginning," Shapiro said. "You may as well sit over here so we can both look at it."

Tony moved his chair and sat beside Shapiro at the small desk. Shapiro had the best of that. He had the kneehole. Of course, it was his desk.

January first that year had come on a Saturday. Presumably, Jo-An had been at the plantation outside Mobile on the first day of her last year. If she had, nothing had occurred worth noting down on the calendar pad.

She had put the sheets for the new year in on top of the last days of the old, as most people do. He flicked to the year before. He came on pencil marks. "Pt J's." Was that what Jo-An meant to write? Or: "Qt P's?"

"If that's a sample of the way she wrote, God help us," Tony said. "Party at somebody named J something? Or a quart of something that begins with P?"

"Anybody's guess," Shapiro said, and flicked pages—blank pages until late in January. On January 28 there was something which might be "Bu del." And as easily be something entirely different. On the sheets of calendar pads people write reminders to themselves. Such reminders are cryptic at the best. In what Jo-An had used for handwriting they were indecipherable. "Buick delivered?" That was Tony's suggestion. If, of course, what looked like a "B" was in fact a "B." It might as well be an "H."

"No wonder she typed her stories," Cook said, as Nathan flicked the year's sheets. Shapiro said that it was possible she had written more clearly when she was not writing only to herself. It was Tony Cook's turn to make the "Mmmm" sound of doubt.

Most of the sheets Shapiro flicked back on their curved supports were blank. If Jo-An Lacey had had engagements, had things she wanted to remember, during February she had not entered them on her calendar pad.

A recluse, Shapiro wondered? Or a woman who lived only at her typewriter—the typewriter to which she was so devoted that her brother had to go down the road for his meals? Nothing for February. Nothing for the first half of March. Then, on March 14, "LS 2." (If it was "LS.") The "2" was reasonably clear. It might, of course, have been a "3."

"Her lawyer was named Sturdevant," Tony said. "Leslie Sturdevant. An appointment with him?"

Shapiro shrugged. He jotted the date and the notation down on a pad of his own. He made it "LS 2" and wrote the characters more clearly, infinitely more clearly, than Jo-An Lacey had written them. He said, "We can give him a ring tomorrow and ask," and flicked on. There was nothing else in March. In early April there was, "JH 2000." If the initials were "JH"; if the figures were "2000."

"John Henry for her brother," Tony suggested. "Two thousand for his pocket?"

"Her checkbook will show," Shapiro said. "When we get to her checkbook."

He flipped on. The remaining days in April had been empty days for Jo-An Lacey. She had written no memos to herself. He came to Friday, the nineteenth of May. And he came to "Lv Uy," or what appeared to be "Lv Uy."

"Love Uriah Yancey?" Tony suggested.

Nathan gave that barely audible "Mmmm." He continued to stare at the sheet in front of him. He said, "About when was she supposed to have come up, Tony?"

"A month or so ago," Tony said. "Five or six weeks ago. Oh."

"Yes," Shapiro said. "It could be she meant 'Leave for New York.' If the 'U' was meant to be an 'N.' By train she probably would have got here the next day. Late the next day. We'll have to check trains."

There was no entry for Saturday, May twentieth, nor for Sunday, the twenty-first. On Monday there was "OK 7:30." Except, of course, that the initials might as easily be "AH."

"Oscar Karn at seven-thirty," Shapiro said. "We'll guess it that way. For dinner, probably. A welcome-to-New-York dinner. For her and her new book. He mentioned taking her to dinner. Said once or twice." He flipped to Tuesday, the twenty-third of May. He came on "M, 2."

The numeral was clear. The "M" might as easily have been "W."

"M for Morton?" Tony said. "Only, he said she came to him only a couple of weeks ago."

Shapiro said, "Mmmm," which seemed to both of them as far as they were getting. But then he pushed the calendar pad toward Tony. He pointed to the letter "M." Tony looked at the sheet and then at Nathan. He shook his head. He said, "Looks like an M to me, Nate."

"An M with a line drawn under it," Shapiro said. "Could be just a slip of the pencil, of course."

"All of them look like slips of the pencil," Tony said. "Of course, nobody writes by hand much any more. She—well, she rather carried it to extremes, didn't she?" He looked down again at the sheet in front of them.

"It does look as if she had drawn a line under the 'M,'" he said. "Intentionally, I mean. Should it mean something? Or just a kind of shorthand to herself?"

"I don't know," Shapiro said. "I've a feeling it ought to mean something but—it just keeps slipping away. Probably it did to her, I suppose." He turned another page. There was a notation on the next page, that of Wednesday, the twenty-fourth of May. Again there were scrawled initials, and again they looked like "OK," and again there could be no certainty. After the initials, there were three letters, in lower case. They appeared to be "1 ex." There appeared to be a space between the "1" and the "ex." (If it was a lower-case "1." If the other letters were "ex.") They both shook their heads. Shapiro turned back to the sheet which had the underlined "M" on it. They looked at each other, and they both shrugged their

127

shoulders and shook their heads. Shapiro flicked on to June.

June had been busier for Jo-An Lacey. There were more initials, with times penciled after them. Some of them were a little clearer than earlier initials had been. On June first, a Thursday, there was "OK, lun" and both the "OK" and the "lun" were clear enough. On that day, Oscar Karn had taken his promising young writer to lunch. They both felt an elation which had no basis in fact. They had found something comprehensible. On the other hand, they already knew that Karn had taken Jo-An to lunch. The date got them no further; it was not really an answer to anything.

Shapiro turned on. Sunday, June fourth. "LS 7 rd bd."

And that, again, was easy enough—if the letters really were "L" and "S." She had had a date with Laurence Shepley, and Laurence Shepley had a red beard.

"A girl I knew once did that sort of thing," Tony said. "Wrote down things about people she met, so she could identify them if she met them again. She showed me one or two. One was a John something. The identifying thing—'Makes wife sick at stomach.' Not especially helpful, I wouldn't have thought."

"Unless your friend always met John something and his wife together," Shapiro said, and flipped through the rest of the week in June. He came on nothing until he reached Friday, the ninth. Then they read, "K's for wkend," and about that there wasn't much doubt. There was also little enlightenment. Karn had said he and his wife had had Jo-An for a weekend at the house near Mount Kisco.

The initials "LS" appeared several times on the sheets for early June—appeared more often, Nathan Shapiro thought, than Laurence Shepley had indicated they would. But Shepley had not been specific. "OK" appeared once again. And on June 12 there was a name which was quite clear; which was printed for clarity. "Phillips Morton." There was also "529 5th" and a telephone number. And one of her dates with Laurence Shepley had been the evening before. June 12 had been a Monday. And on the following day the writing again was clear enough: "Shwd PM con." Again the meaning was, they agreed, clear enough.

There were no entries on the sheets for the rest of June.

Shapiro flicked back to the sheet which had the underlined "M" on it—the "M" followed by a "2." (If it was a "2.") It ought to mean something. He looked at Tony Cook and pointed a finger at the "M" with a line under it. Tony shook his head. "Not Morton," he said. "She hadn't met him then. Somebody we haven't come across?"

Shapiro lifted his shoulders and let them subside again. He continued to look at the sheet he had turned to. Then he reached for the telephone and dialed. He waited some minutes for an answer.

Tony Cook didn't ask him anything.

"My wife," Nathan Shapiro said. "Probably out walking the dog. Her doctorate is in English literature. I don't know whether that includes orthography, but could be it does."

He tapped his fingers on the desk top. He looked at the watch on his wrist. He put Jo-An's calendar pad in his pocket.

"I think," Nathan said, "we may as well knock it off for today. For what remains of it. Maybe we'll be fresher tomorrow. Maybe something will turn up tomorrow."

There was very little hope in his voice. But Tony Cook has got used to that.

There was a cruising cab in Twenty-third Street. It had "Air Conditioned" on a window. Nathan Shapiro thought of the heat of the subway, of the infrequency of trains on a Sunday. He succumbed to temptation and flagged down the cab. He said to Tony, "Drop you?" Tony shook his head. Shapiro gave the cab driver the address.

"That's Brooklyn," the hacker said, his tone accusing. "I don't go to Brooklyn, mister. Anyways, I'm due at the garage."

Nathan Shapiro is usually gentle with cab drivers. He was not, this hot afternoon of a fruitless day—and a day which was supposed to have been an off-duty day—Shapiro felt no gentleness.

"No off-duty sign," he told the cab driver. "And you'll go where I say."

"So," the driver said. "A tough guy. Wants to make something out of it."

Shapiro took his shield out of his pocket, and the hacker turned in his seat and looked at it. He said, "O.K. You've made something out of it," and put the car in gear.

It was reasonably cool in the Brooklyn apartment, and Rose had got home from walking Cleo. She wore a sleeveless summer dress, and when Nathan went into the living room she was up and moving toward him. She had left a paperback turned down on a table near the window she had been sitting by. She looked up at him and looked for some seconds and then shook her head. She said, "Sit down and take off your gun. I'll get us something cold."

"It's too—" Nathan said, and Rose, on her way to the kitchen, said over her shoulder, "It's not too for anything, dear. Take your gun off."

He took his gun off. He sat on the sofa in front of the fireplace. He took Jo-An's calendar pad out of his pocket and opened it on his lap. Rose came back with two tall glasses with ice and liquid in them, and this time the liquid in both was the color of water. It bubbled in both glasses.

"Gin and tonic," Rose said. "I think you need it, darling."

She put the two glasses down on the coffee table in front of the sofa and sat beside Nathan. They clicked glasses and sipped from them. The gin and tonic was cold and pungent, and Nathan thought only briefly of his stomach. What he thought was, The hell with it. For this once, the hell with it. Rose said, "Whose calendar pad, Nathan?"

"The dead girl's," Nathan said. "Her handwriting's terrible."

"Her real writing isn't," Rose said. "I've been reading her. Her famous one. Mike had it in paperback." She pointed toward the book on the table by the window. "She's very good, dear. Now and then almost magically good. It's—it's almost a tragedy she was killed."

"It's almost a tragedy when anyone's killed," Nathan said, but she shook her head at him.

130

"Sad," Rose said. "Distressing. Tragedy is for greatness. She —I think she almost had it, Nathan. Think she might have had it. Are you and Tony Cook getting anywhere?"

He closed sad eyes for a moment and shook his head.

"You will," she told him.

He shook his head again. He took another sip of his drink. He flicked the calendar pad open to the entry of Tuesday, the twenty-third of May—to the "M" with a line under it and the numeral "2." He held it toward Rose.

"She certainly scrawled," Rose said. "We try to teach them not to, but nothing much comes of it. Of course, nowadays most of them just print. Script is a vanishing art."

Rose is a schoolteacher by profession. She was, that year, the assistant principal of a high school in Greenwich Village.

"Is it supposed to mean something?" Rose asked, and pointed at the "M, 2."

"We haven't worked anything out," Nathan said. "Just a letter and a figure. And a letter which might be an M and might as easily be a W."

"Oh, no," Rose said. "A W, of course. That's why the line's under it."

He turned to look at her. He raised his eyebrows.

"Of course," she said again. "In handwritten copy, you put a line under a W and over an M. For the printer. It's the same with the U and the N. Because as many people write it's hard to tell them apart. Proofreaders. Headline writers. People who have to make longhand corrections. A W, not an M, dear. Probably she made longhand corrections in typescript. That sort of thing. And got into the habit."

He looked again at the three sheets of Jo-An Lacey's memo pad. Dinner with (presumably) OK on Monday, the twenty-second of May. "W, 2" on the following day. And on the day after, "OK" again with "1 ex" after it. He shook his head. He sipped from the tall glass. He looked at Rose and shook his head again.

"Somebody whose name begins with W," Rose said. "An appointment at two o'clock in the afternoon? Is there somebody whose name begins with W on your list, dear?"

131

"No," Nathan told her. "She may, of course, have known any number of people whose names began with W. We've no idea who she knew. Her publisher. A man named Laurence Shepley. Her brother, who's showed up. She may have known a hundred people in New York. People named Williams and Wingate and, for all we know, Weinstein. She could have had an engagement with any of—"

He stopped. He looked thoughtfully at the portrait of his father over the mantelpiece. The dark eyes of the portrait, eyes so like his own, seemed to look back at him, in rather somber thought.

"Two o'clock in the afternoon," Nathan said. "If that's what the figure '2' is for. Hardly two in the morning. Two in the afternoon is late for a luncheon date. Too early for a cocktail date. What would two people be doing at two in the afternoon?"

"Any number of things," Rose said. "Going to a movie. Taking a walk. On Saturdays, when you're working, I take naps. When I haven't got things piled up at the office. It's amazing how things—"

She stopped. She looked intently at her husband's long, sad face.

"An office," Nathan said. "Two in the afternoon would be a reasonable time to have an appointment at somebody's office. At the office of somebody whose name begins with—"

He broke off. He looked, not at the portrait of his father but at his wife. There was, Rose thought, a difference in his eyes.

"A lawyer's office?" Shapiro said. "To make out her will? As Karn had advised her to the night before?" He shook his head. "Which is only guessing," he said. "Stabbing in the dark. Only—"

He flipped to the next page and held it out to Rose. "'OK' for Karn," he said. "'L ex' for what, Rose?"

She looked at "l ex." She shook her head.

"An abbreviation for 'literary executor,'" Nathan said. "It's all still guessing, of course. Oscar Karn named that in the will she'd had drawn up the day before. By some lawyer Karn gave her the name of?"

132

Rose nodded her head.

"We've heard of two lawyers so far," Nathan said. "One's an old guy—apparently a crusty old guy—Tony talked to in Mobile. And didn't get much out of. The other's a man Tony ran into last night at a party with Rachel Farmer. A man named—" He stopped and shook his head for an instant. It came to him. "Carson," he said. "Alvin Carson. He's representing something called the Jefferson Press in negotiations about a merger of that and Oscar Karn, Incorporated. Negotiating, I suppose, with Karn's lawyers. Damn Sundays."

"Why, dear?"

"Because in summer nobody's at home on them," he said. "And offices are all closed. Still—"

He finished his drink. He got up and went to the shelf where the telephone directories were piled—directories for Manhattan and Brooklyn and the rest, including Westchester County. A detective has no idea where he may need to call.

Shapiro brought the Manhattan directory back to the sofa. Rose had taken both glasses back to the kitchen. Perhaps, if she brought them back filled, his would, this time, be filled with sweet wine and soda. Not that the gin and tonic seemed to be annoying his stomach.

"Carson." A lot of Carsons. "Carson Fuller & Steinbeck attys." Back up the column. "Carson Alvin atty"; and, in the next line, "Residence" in the East Seventies. Carson wouldn't be there on a sunny Sunday afternoon. Carson would be somewhere playing golf. Or somewhere swimming. Or somewhere in the country sitting in a shady place. Still—

He went to the telephone and dialed. He waited for several rings. He got, "The Carson residence." The voice was female, with an accent. He thought German.

"I'd like to speak to Mr. Carson," Shapiro said. "If he happens to be at home."

"I don't know," the maid said. "If it's about business, that would be his office." The 'would' was a little like 'voud.' "I'll go find out, though. Mister?"

"Shapiro. Nathan Shapiro. It's Lieutenant Shapiro, tell Mr. Carson. And that I'll only keep him a minute."

133

"I see," the maid said. "You vait."

Shapiro waited. He waited for several minutes. Then he heard, "Carson, Lieutenant. What can I do for you?"

The voice was level, entirely impartial.

"Perhaps give me a name," Shapiro said. "Sorry to bother you on a Sunday afternoon, but it might be important. In connection with an investigation we're carrying on."

"Into the death of Miss Jo-An Lacey," Carson said. "I supposed that. Ran into this side-kick of yours at a party downtown. What name?"

"You're representing the Jefferson Press in merger negotiations with the Karn company," Shapiro said. "At least, that's what I hear."

"Right."

"The name of your opposite number," Shapiro said. "The lawyer representing the Karn interests."

"Why? Not that there's any secret about it. Littlejohn and Williams. Norm Littlejohn, primarily. Norman Littlejohn. Why?"

"I want to ask him a question which he probably won't want to answer," Shapiro said. "Nothing to do with the merger, Mr. Carson."

"Norman Littlejohn," Carson said again. "Lives up in Westchester some place. Or spends weekends there anyway. God knows why anybody'd want to."

Prejudices draw people together. Shapiro felt kinship with Alvin Carson. Prospect Park provides adequate open space for Nathan Shapiro.

"Do you happen to know," Shapiro said, "whether Mr. Littlejohn generally represents Mr. Karn? Or is he—his firm, I mean—only concerned with this proposed merger?"

"Far's I know," Carson said, "Littlejohn and Williams are general counsel for Karn. What's it all about, Lieutenant? Miss Lacey, I suppose?"

"It may be," Shapiro said. "I can't go beyond that, Mr. Carson. Sorry to have interrupted your afternoon."

"I was just watching a ball game," Carson said, "and the Mets are getting clobbered. Anything else I can help you with?"

134

Shapiro said there wasn't and thanked Carson again and hung up.

Rose came back with two tall glasses. The liquid was bubbly and much the color of water. She put the glasses down, and Shapiro looked at them and then at Rose.

"It was supposed," she said, "to be your day off. We were supposed to go walking in the park."

Nathan agreed that there was that. They clicked glasses, as they always did, and Nathan put his glass down and went to get the Westchester County directory. Not that Norman Littlejohn wouldn't be out on a golf course. Or, if he was young enough, on a tennis court.

12

Somewhere in Westchester County a telephone rang. It was not clear where in Westchester; the address listed in the directory was cryptic—as cryptic, almost, as the entries on Jo-An Lacey's calendar pad. The address was "Cres Ct." Shapiro let the telephone ring. He was not especially hopeful; Norman Littlejohn probably was not at home this warm Sunday afternoon. Probably he was at a country club. But he might be merely outside on a shady terrace, with a long drink on a table beside him.

When the answer came it was "Yes?" in a woman's voice. And yes, this was the Littlejohns'. Then, "This is Lois Littlejohn."

"Mr. Littlejohn?"

"I'm afraid not. And won't be—oh, for hours, probably."

"Have you any idea where I can reach him, Mrs. Littlejohn?"

The last was a guess. Lois Littlejohn might, of course, be a daughter. But there was maturity in the soft voice.

"I can take a message," Lois Littlejohn said. "Give it to him when he gets home, as he will sometime. As I guess he will sometime."

"I'm a police lieutenant," Shapiro said. "Point or two we think Mr. Littlejohn might help us with."

"About that poor girl," Lois said. "But how could he help, Lieutenant?"

"Shapiro."

She repeated his name, again with a question in her voice.

"It is in relation to Miss Lacey," Shapiro said. "And I don't know that he can help. We're just—call it casting around."

"We only just met her," Mrs. Littlejohn said. "Oss had us in for a drink when she was up here. Us and quite a few people. Of course, it was very interesting to meet someone like her. But it was only to—well, say hello. And how much we'd enjoyed her books. The sort of thing people say, you know. As a matter of fact, it was true enough. About enjoying her books, I mean. But that was all either of us knew about her, Lieutenant. So I don't see how—"

She let it hang for him to reach out for.

"I'm not at all sure I do," Shapiro said. "Just an outside chance. We have to take outside chances quite a lot."

She was sure he did. She was also sure Norm would want to help in any way he could.

"The thing is," she said, "he's gone into town. To his office. On such a lovely day. But it's the way he is. He won't bring his work home over weekends. He thinks it's a bad thing to do and so do I. So he goes in where his work is. And leaves me to my own devices, which I'm afraid aren't many. Is this help he might give you urgent, Lieutenant?"

"I don't know that, either," Shapiro told her. "Do you suppose I could call him at his office? I wouldn't need to interrupt him for more than a few minutes."

"You can try," she said. "It's just possible he may have had the phone plugged through. But probably you'll just get the answering service. And the news that the office will be open after nine-thirty tomorrow."

She had no idea when her husband might be home. It might be for dinner; she hoped it would be for dinner. It might be "all hours." Of course she would tell him that Lieutenant Shapiro had called and would like to be called back and where could Lieutenant Shapiro be reached? At police headquarters?

Shapiro gave the telephone number of his apartment and

137

waited while she wrote it down. And, as she carried friendly cooperation further, wrote down the telephone number of the offices of Littlejohn & Williams when she gave it to him—gave it with the regretful assurance that it probably wouldn't do him any good. He thanked her for being so helpful and hung up.

"Your drink's getting warm," Rose said. "No luck, I take it?"

"Not much," Nathan told her and went back and drank from his glass. It wasn't urgent, obviously. It could just as well go over until tomorrow. Only, when you've got hold of an end of a string which, pulled on, might do something about a knot you felt like going on pulling it.

He did get halfway down his drink before he went back to the telephone. Rose sighed at his back. It was a sigh of resignation. Probably, Nathan thought as he spun the dial, Mrs. Lois Littlejohn had sighed so when her husband had said he had to leave "Cres Ct," wherever it might be, and go to his office in the city.

Shapiro waited for four rings. He got, "Littlejohn and Williams, good afternoon."

The voice was professional. It was also a little weary. It was the voice of a young woman stuck with a Sunday duty watch.

Shapiro knew it wouldn't do him any good, but he asked to speak to Mr. Littlejohn.

"The office will be closed until nine-thirty tomorrow morning, sir. This is the answering service."

All right. There wasn't any urgency. Tomorrow would do as well. He went back and sat again beside Rose on the sofa. He drank from his glass. He got the Manhattan directory again. The offices of Littlejohn & Williams, "lwyrs," were in the East Forties; just from the number, beyond Fifth.

Nathan finished his drink and looked up at the portrait of his father and the dark eyes of the portrait seemed to look back at him.

Rose looked at him. Rose said, "Damn it, Nathan." And Nathan Shapiro shook his head and said, "I know, dear," and got up to buckle on his gun.

Rose Shapiro again said, "Damn." She said it with defeat in her voice. She said, "At least take a cab, dear."

138

Nathan promised he would take a cab if he could find one.

He did find one. It was not air-conditioned, but lightning cannot be expected to strike twice on the same afternoon. There was little traffic on the Brooklyn streets and not much more in Manhattan. There were not even many cars parked along the curbs in East Forty-first Street between Fifth and Madison. The cabbie knocked his flag down in front of a tall office building and Nathan paid the fare and the tip.

There was a uniformed guard in the lobby of the building. He got up from his chair when Shapiro went in. He said, "Sir?" politely but with doubt. Shapiro showed him his shield, to save time. The guard said, "O.K. But I'll have to ask you to sign in, anyway. It's the rule nowadays, Lieutenant."

Shapiro signed in. There was a place marked "Purpose." In it Shapiro wrote, "Littlejohn & Williams." The guard looked over his shoulder. He said, "I think Mr. Littlejohn is in his office, sir. Maybe I'd better call up?"

"By all means," Nathan told him. "And if you get Mr. Littlejohn tell him I won't bother him for more than a few minutes."

The guard used a telephone. He came back. He said, "He says O.K. What he said was, 'O.K., for God's sake.' It's on the eighth floor. Damn near all of the eighth floor. Take that one."

He pointed toward an elevator. Shapiro went to it and into it and pushed the button numbered 8. The elevator closed its door and shot upward. It stopped suddenly and opened its door. Across from the elevator was a door with LITTLEJOHN & WILLIAMS, ATTORNEYS AT LAW on it. There was a button in the doorjamb and Shapiro pushed it. Almost at once there was a shadow on the glass, and then the door opened.

The man who opened it was tall and gray-haired and in his shirt sleeves. He looked at Shapiro for a moment, thoughtfully. He said, "You're the one had Fred call up?"

"Yes. Police lieutenant. Shouldn't have to bother you for more than a few minutes, Mr. Littlejohn."

"Police lieutenant?" Littlejohn said. "Name of?"

Nathan gave his name. He also showed his shield.

"Have to be careful nowadays," Littlejohn said. "Planting

139

bombs all over the place, they are. You people ought to do something about it."

"We try," Shapiro said. "Now and then we do. Any outfits here anybody'd want to bomb?"

"God knows," Littlejohn said. "Lawyers mostly, but God knows. Come on in, Lieutenant."

Littlejohn led the way through a general office, with chairs and sofas for waiting clients. He led the way along a corridor and into a large office with windows on two sides of it and a big desk half covered with legal-size papers, most of them in neat piles. Littlejohn went behind the desk and shuffled loose papers in front of him into a pile. He said, "So, Lieutenant?"

"A month or so ago," Shapiro said, "did a Miss Jo-An Lacey come to your office? At, perhaps, the suggestion of Mr. Oscar Karn? And did she come to have you draw up a will?"

Littlejohn said, "Oh, that's what it's about."

"Yes," Shapiro said. "That's what it's about, sir. And it's only fair to tell you we're more or less just guessing."

"You're in charge of the investigation of Miss Lacey's death, Lieutenant?"

"The chief of detectives is in charge of it, Mr. Littlejohn. It comes on down the line. Through the officer commanding Homicide South. To me, among others. Among a lot of others. Yours isn't a criminal practice, I take it?"

"Good God, no," Littlejohn said. "You smoke cigars, Lieutenant?" He got a box of cigars out of a desk drawer before Nathan had a chance to say no thanks, he didn't smoke cigars. Littlejohn took a cigar from the box and clipped the end off it and lighted it. He took his time about it. He was taking time, Shapiro decided, to think.

Littlejohn blew smoke toward the ceiling. He said, "I suppose you understand about privileged communications, Lieutenant?"

"Yes. And that Miss Lacey is dead, Counselor."

"And that, in due course, any will she may have made will be filed for probate? And that when probate is granted, the will will be available to interested parties?"

"Yes, Counselor."

140

"But you're trying a short-cut?"

There was no testiness in the gray-haired man's voice; no annoyance in his deeply tanned face. He spoke as one merely seeking to satisfy curiosity.

"Yes, Counselor. Just trying to get on with the investigation. To—well, to keep things from dragging out."

"Shapiro," Littlejohn said. "Haven't I heard of you?"

"Possibly. Sometimes names get into the newspapers."

"There was an actress killed down in the Village a while back," Littlejohn said. "Someone I knew slightly years ago. Your name was in the newspapers in connection with that case, wasn't it?"

"Yes."

"And a painter—a fairly famous one—killed in his studio? Also downtown?"

"Yes, Counselor. And the painter named Shackleford Jones."

"You seem to have got your man both times," Littlejohn said, and blew smoke at the ceiling. The smoke was fragrant.

Shapiro got a pack of cigarettes out of his pocket and lighted a cigarette. He said, "Yes, Counselor. One time it was a woman, but yes."

"Miss Jo-An Lacey came to the office late in May," Littlejohn said. "I've forgotten the exact date."

"The twenty-third, we think," Shapiro said.

"Oss Karn had suggested us," Littlejohn said. "We're general counsel for Oscar Karn, Incorporated. Natural he'd suggest us, of course. She wanted to make out a will. You were right about that. It was a very simple will. It revoked any previous will. We drew it up. She signed it before witnesses. 'In her presence and the presence of each other,' according to the formula."

"You have it here, Mr. Littlejohn?"

"In the vault. With a time lock on it. It won't be available until nine-thirty tomorrow morning."

"You drew it up yourself, Mr. Littlejohn. Or was it somebody else in the firm?"

"Oss is an old friend of mine," Littlejohn said. "He suggested my name, specifically. Yes, I drew it up."

141

Shapiro didn't say anything. He drew on his cigarette and blew smoke ceilingward to join the fragrant cigar smoke.

"Very simple," Littlejohn said. "Not more than a page, in spite of all the verbiage required. Being of sound mind. Revoking all other wills. That sort of thing. Everything to her brother. And he the executor."

"Have you any idea what the 'everything' would add up to, Counselor?"

"No. None of our concern. Could be a dime. Could be a million. Whatever it is, this brother of hers—I'm not sure I remember his name. John something."

"John Henry Lacey," Shapiro said. "And he's the executor?"

"Yes."

"By himself? I mean, sometimes there are several executors. Isn't that right?"

"Sometimes. Depends on the wishes of the testator."

"And her brother was the only executor?"

"Oh, Oss Karn is in as her literary executor. More or less a formality. Knows his way around in the field. After all, it's his field. Has been for years. Miss Lacey thought he might advise her brother about her—" He paused and drew on his cigar and let the smoke out. "Literary remains," he said.

"So Mr. Karn would have a say in the disposition of any writing she—left behind."

"That'll be up to Lacey," Littlejohn said. "Karn's role would be merely advisory. Lacey will be quite free to disregard it."

"Pending probate," Shapiro said, "what can Lacey do about whatever literary property his sister left him?"

"Strictly, not much. Oh, he can negotiate, of course. Sign some contingent agreement, if he wants to. If you mean a formal contract for publication, not until the will goes through."

Shapiro said he saw. He said that Mr. Littlejohn had made things entirely clear. He ground his cigarette out and stood up. Littlejohn said, "All you want, Lieutenant?"

"All you can give me, Counselor," Shapiro said. "Damn good of you to spare me so much time."

"I'm an officer of the court," Littlejohn said.

"You could have held out," Shapiro said. "Not that there's

142

much to hold out on, of course. But we appreciate it that you didn't."

"What you expected, Lieutenant?"

"Pretty much," Shapiro said and then, much to his own surprise, added: "Your wife hopes you'll get home for dinner."

Littlejohn laughed. There was a sudden gaiety in his laughter.

"And so do I, Lieutenant," Littlejohn said. "So very much do I."

He went with Shapiro to the door of the outer office. When Shapiro was outside it, he heard the lock click behind him. On the street, a cruising cab tempted him. He resisted the temptation. He walked to Grand Central and waited, on a sparsely populated platform, for an express to Brooklyn. Two young men, both with long hair and both wearing blue jeans, were among the others waiting for a train. When Shapiro came down the stairs to the express platform, they looked at him and then, a little abruptly, walked away. They walked up the stairs Shapiro had come down. Nathan Shapiro had no memory of having seen either of them before. They, he thought, had better memories. Or perhaps it was merely that he looked like a policeman.

The express he wanted came, finally. It was hot, but it had been hot on the platform. There were, however, seats in the car. And, finally, the train took him to Brooklyn; finally he climbed the stairs to his apartment. It was cool in the apartment, and Rose put her book opened on a table. The book still was *Snake Country* by Jo-An Lacey. Rose seemed to be almost halfway through it.

"You weren't as long as I thought you'd be, dear," Rose said. "Which is a nice change. Did the Lacey girl make a will?"

Nathan took his jacket off and unbuckled his gun. Rose said, "Good. At last."

Nathan said that the Lacey girl had made a will, and that Norman Littlejohn had been very accommodating, as lawyers went. Rose said she would get them something cold. Iced tea? Or iced coffee? Or, of course—

The telephone rang and Rose said, "Damn," and went to-

143

ward the kitchen. Nathan picked the telephone up and said, "Shapiro," and in his own ears his voice sounded limp and tired.

"I'm sorry to keep breaking in on you," Tony Cook said. "And probably it doesn't get us anywhere. Only, I'm at Rachel's apartment and I was—well, I guess I was talking too much. About the Lacey case."

"We all do," Nathan said. "To people we trust. So?"

"I described this John Henry Lacey to her," Tony said. "Laid it on a little, I suppose. The Old South, down to the accent—the wispy blond beard and the seersucker suit. And that he was looking for grits. Oh, the works. Of course, verbal descriptions—well, they aren't really much good, as we both know too damn well. But—"

He paused. Nathan thought that, probably, he had looked at Rachel Farmer and been momentarily distracted. After a second or so, Nathan said, "Yes, Tony?"

"Rachel thinks he sounds like a man she saw. Walking through Gay Street, when she was going the other way—coming home, actually. Tall and thin and light-colored hair and a little chin beard. And, wearing a seersucker suit. A sort of scraggly beard, as she remembers it. A sort of weedy man, she says he was. It probably doesn't get us anywhere, but for what it's worth. The thing is," Tony said, "Rachel saw this man, who just could be our Southern gentleman, in Gay Street a week ago. A week ago, or perhaps a little longer ago. And he only got into town yesterday, according to what he says."

Shapiro hesitated. He said, "Just from your description, Tony?" and got "Yes" for an answer; got also, "I know it's damn vague, Nate. Only—well, Rachel looks at people. Remembers people. I thought—"

"Yes," Shapiro said. "It would be interesting if Lacey was in town a week or so ago. He inherits all his sister's money, as it turns out. A good deal of money, probably. It's too bad Lacey's up in the country, because—"

He said, "Wait a minute, Tony. Or—say I'll call you back. You and Miss Farmer going to be in her place for a while?"

"We're having a drink," Tony Cook said. "Eventually, we'll go out to dinner. Not—right away."

"I'll check on something," Shapiro said. "Call you back. Oh, and give our best to Miss Farmer."

Cook said, "Sure," and hung up. Shapiro dialed the office. He got, "Homicide South, Detective Farwell." Farwell would certainly see, Lieutenant.

He was gone a few minutes. He came back. He said, "Nothing too hot, far's I can tell. The precinct people have pretty much covered Gay Street. Forty-seventh Street's pretty much covered the Algonquin. Nothing much seems to be turning up."

"The State Police? Up in Westchester? The Karn place?"

"Memo on that," Farwell said. "Matter of fact, I took it myself. Subject's apparently on his way back to town. Subject being?"

"Lacey," Shapiro told him. "Being driven back by Mr. Karn? Or didn't they say?"

"Being driven back by Karn's chauffeur," Farwell said. "Man —wait a minute, Lieutenant. Man named Stokes. Karn isn't along, according to the trooper who called. I guess that's all's come in, Na—sir."

Nathan said, "Thanks," and hung up. He dialed again at once. Tony Cook answered.

"When you and Miss Farmer go out to dinner," Shapiro said, "did you plan to go some place in the neighborhood?"

"We haven't decided, Nate. Rachel says she's got a steak and—"

"Has she got a freezer?"

"Sure."

"Ask her to put the steak in it," Nathan said. "Take her up to dinner at the Algonquin. O.K.? Put it on the expense account, if you like."

"No," Tony said. "Sure we'll go there, if you say so. Not at the expense of the department. Why, Nate?"

"There's just a chance," Shapiro said, "that Miss Farmer may see somebody she's seen before. Lacey seems to be on his way back to town. Presumably to the Algonquin. Maybe just to pick up his luggage, of course. Maybe not. Maybe he'll have dinner there."

"He won't get grits, I shouldn't think," Tony said. "We'll have dinner at the Algonquin. And drinks in the lobby. And Rachel will keep her eyes open."

"Good," Nathan said. "And what the hell are grits?"

"Hominy grits," Tony said. "People in the South eat them, apparently. Sort of like porridge, at a guess. I never tried them myself. We'll be at the Algonquin as soon as Rachel puts her clo—what I mean is, she'll want to dress up some if we're going out. Instead of staying in, I mean."

Puts her clothes on, Tony was going to say before he got flustered, Nathan thought, and he thought it was a wonder that Tony, in the presence of Rachel with no clothes on, had been making as much sense as he had. Not that it was any of Nathan's business how two attractive people played. But he felt momentarily cheered. He went back to the sofa in front of the fireplace and sipped iced coffee. He looked at the portrait of his father. He got up, and Rose shook her head sadly and lighted a cigarette.

Nathan went back to the telephone. This one would have to go through channels. For Nathan Shapiro, the channel started with Captain William Weigand, Commanding, Homicide South. The office would know Weigand's whereabouts, but he might as well try the Weigands' apartment first. He dialed.

Dorian Weigand answered the telephone. She said, "Yes, he is, Nathan. We were just sitting watching the boats."

The Weigand apartment overlooks the East River. In it you can sit in front of a big window and watch tugs towing barges, or pushing barges.

Bill Weigand said, "Yes, Nate?" and listened. He said, "Yes, we'd better. Seersucker suit? A taste for something called grits? Right."

"Of course," Shapiro said, "he may have changed his clothes."

"Yes," Weigand said, "he may have changed his clothes, Nate. I'll get it started."

146

What Weigand got started were the feet of detectives from several precinct squads. He got them plodding into the lobbies and up to the desks of hotels, beginning with those nearest Pennsylvania Station, into which a stranger to town might most easily wander. They were not armed with much—not with photographs, only with a somewhat shadowy description. A tall thin man, perhaps wearing a seersucker suit? A man with a Southern accent? A man who, if he had eaten breakfast at the hotel—had breakfast sent to his room or gone to the coffee shop for it—might have asked for grits? A man who might have had for luggage only one heavy suitcase? A man with a wispy chin beard? A man who might have checked in a week ago or ten days ago?

Police work is like that. It requires a lot of walking; the asking of a lot of questions which are not likely to be answered. A photograph would have helped; probably the detective from the District Attorney's Homicide Bureau who had flown down to Mobile, Alabama, as soon as Jo-An's body had been identified would turn up photographs, including one of John Henry Lacey III. If he did, he would wire it up. In that case, the detectives plodding from hotel to hotel could plod all over again.

Shapiro finished his coffee. He looked at his watch and found that it was almost six o'clock of the Sunday evening. He said, "What do you say we go out to dinner? Over to Manhattan, say. To make up for the walk in the park we didn't get to take."

"Oh," Rose said, "I've got—"

She looked at her husband. She didn't say what she'd got for dinner. She said, "I think that's a fine idea, dear. I'll change, but it won't be a minute. Meanwhile—"

She looked at him again.

"Why, darling," Rose said, "don't you wear your other suit?"

Nathan looked down at himself. The suit looked all right to him. Perhaps it did need a little pressing. So, as far as he remembered, would the other suit. "Sure," Nathan said. "I'll even put on a clean shirt."

They changed. The other suit was pressed. Rose had taken care of that. They got a cab more quickly than they had any

147

right to expect. Shapiro said, "The Algonquin. It's on Forty-fourth Street between Sixth and Fifth."

"The Avenue of the Americas," the hacker said. "Sure thing, Mac."

They had gone several blocks and been stopped by a light before Rose said that she had a feeling, and Nathan said, "What kind of feeling, Rose?"

"That on Sunday nights in summer a lot of hotels close their restaurants," Rose said. "I don't know about the Algonquin. But probably they still sell drinks."

"What about the people who live there?" Shapiro said.

"Oh, go somewhere that's open," Rose told him. "Or perhaps there's still room service. We may have to get a room for overnight. To get dinner."

13

There were people having drinks in the lobby of the Hotel Algonquin. It was not as crowded as it had been the other time Shapiro had been in it. The doors to the Rose Room were open, but those to the Oak Room were closed. One of the people in the lobby was a slender young woman with long blond hair. She was sitting by herself in a deep chair from which she could see around most of the big room and also see the elevators. In front of her on a small table was a glass which, from its shape, contained sherry.

"She looks like somebody we know a little," Rose said, and Nathan, who had merely glanced at first, looked again. The slender young woman looked at him—she seemed to be looking at everybody—but showed no sign she had ever seen him before. Shapiro's expression was equally blank. He said, "There's one," and they went to a sofa behind the big clock. They tinkled the bell and Rose looked at her husband and said, "What's so funny, dear?"

Nobody else, looking at Nathan Shapiro, would have thought there was anything funny; to most he would have looked as sad as always.

"Rachel Farmer," Nathan said. "Doing it up brown. Or, actually, doing it up blond. Miss Farmer with a wig, dear. And Tony—" Nathan looked around the room. "Yes," he said. "Over

149

there in the corner, behind a copy of something called *Variety*."

A waiter said, "Sir? Madam?"

Rose said, "A very dry martini, please." Nathan said, "A sherry. Not too dry." He added the last with no special sound of hope in his voice.

The waiter went away.

"Probably," Nathan said, "the wig was Miss Farmer's idea." He leaned forward and twisted a little so that he could see Rachel Farmer in her blond wig. She seemed to be regarding the elevators. She reached forward and picked up her little glass and sipped from it.

"The wig looks bunchy, somehow," Shapiro said.

Rose explained that. Rachel had let her own hair grow long. Her own hair was bunched under the wig. Rose thought the wig looked very natural, considering. And that Rachel probably had assorted wigs—accouterments of her profession. "Sometimes," Rose said, "photographers may also prefer blondes. Now, of course, because if she recognizes the man she's supposed to recognize, he might recognize her. And—"

Their drinks came and a check with them. Nathan put a bill on the tray with the check. He said, "Do you serve dinner on Sundays?" The waiter said, "No, sir. Sorry, sir. Thank you, sir," and carried the tray away.

"The traffic will be bad on Sunday afternoon," Rose said. "On a summer Sunday afternoon. I wonder why—" She stopped, because Nathan was not listening. He was looking toward the almost-head-high partition which shields those drinking in the Algonquin lobby from those who are going into and out of the hotel. If those moving either way are tall enough, their heads are visible. Rose looked as Nathan was looking. She saw a head with rather sparse blond hair and a scraggly chin beard. She looked at Nathan, and Nathan nodded.

In front of the desk, just visible from where they sat, a body became attached to the head. It was a long, thin body, in a noticeably unpressed seersucker suit. Nathan Shapiro leaned and twisted so that he could see Rachel in her blond wig. She had lifted her sherry glass but was looking beyond it. She was looking expectantly, Shapiro thought, as if an overdue date were being waited for. She was looking at, among others, John Henry Lacey III, returned from the country. There was no change in her expression.

Lacey picked up his room key and went to the elevator. There he turned, as he waited, and looked over the lobby. The Shapiros were out of his view; Tony Cook was behind *Variety*. Rachel bent her head a little as she lifted her glass again and sipped from it. The elevator door opened and people came out of the car, and Lacey waited and went into it. The door closed on him.

Rachel stood and shook her head, indignantly—a woman who had been stood up and who was fed with it. Tony folded his copy of *Variety* and tucked it into his chair and went around the end of the shielding partition and then along the corridor it formed between the Blue Bar and the desk and the lobby. Rachel met him halfway with an "It's high time" expression on her face.

"There ought really to be footlights," Rose said.

"They're young," Nathan said. "For the young there ought always to be time for games."

Tony put an arm around Rachel's shoulders. He kissed her lightly on the cheek. He guided her around the grandfather clock to the sofa where the Shapiros were sitting. Nathan stood up.

"Didn't know you planned to sit in," Tony said, and Rachel said, "Good evening, Lieutenant. Hi, Rose. This damned thing's too tight. It's giving me a headache. The answer is yes, I'm almost sure."

The sofa was wide enough for the four of them.

"Pretty sure?" Nathan said. "Or really very sure? And how long ago?"

"He stands out in a funny sort of way," Rachel said. "By not looking as if he belonged here. He didn't belong in Gay Street, either. Yes, I'm pretty sure. All right, very sure. And it was a week ago. Perhaps a little more than a week ago." She turned to Tony. "Can I take this damn thing off now, mister?" she asked him.

"If you don't go back to calling me 'mister,'" Tony said. "And it was your idea, darling. Just pull it—"

"No," Shapiro said. "Wait until we're outside, if you don't mind. Lacey may decide to come down and go out to dinner." He tapped the bell. The waiter returned; he was very quick, because the number of customers had diminished. A very dry martini, a very dry sherry, a not-so-dry sherry, and a bourbon on the rocks.

"They don't serve dinner on Sundays," Rachel said. "I was invited to dinner, mis—Tony. And when I bought this wig, I wore my own hair short. Bought it to sit on the back of a motorcycle, holding on to the man in front, with long blond tresses blowing back. And the fan almost blew me off the seat."

She fidgeted with her blond wig, trying to ease its pressure on her forehead.

"Advertising the motorcycle?" Rose asked.

"Some toothpaste or other," Rachel said. "I had my mouth open, from the joy and excitement of it all. There was special lighting on my teeth. Took them almost three hours to get it just right. Good." The last was to the waiter who brought them drinks.

Shapiro lifted his and put it down without tasting it. He got up and went through the sparsely populated lobby. He stopped at the desk and asked something and got an answer and nodded his head. He went to one of the telephone booths and closed himself into it. He was there several minutes and came back and sat down again.

"Precinct will get a man over," he said, speaking chiefly to Tony Cook. "Man named Fleming. Ever run into him, Tony?"

"If his first name is Frederick," Tony said. "Old F.F. He's been around for years. Good man, for all I know. We wait for him?"

"I think so," Shapiro said. "Sorry, Miss Farmer. About the wig, I mean. It shouldn't be long. Then—then we can all go somewhere to dinner. Unless you and Tony?"

Rachel and Tony Cook looked at each other, briefly.

"The four of us would be fine," Rachel said.

"We can go down to Charles," Tony said.

152

"I hope he comes soon," Rachel said. "The way this thing's cutting into me, I'll be marked for life."

They drank, Rachel fingering the wig from time to time.

Nathan's sherry wasn't really the way he likes sherry.

It was only about ten minutes before a gray-haired, rather stocky man, apparently in his fifties, walked into the lobby and looked around it, as though for an empty table. There were plenty of empty tables. He looked at the Shapiros and at Rachel and Tony. It was obvious from his expression that he had never seen them before. He chose a chair which faced the elevators and tinkled the bell on it.

"Fleming," Tony said. "To take over the watch."

"He spotted us," Shapiro said. "So we can drink up and go."

They drank up and paid and went. They had to go in two taxis, since New York taxicabs no longer carry four, except when, once in a hundred times or so, a survivor from a brighter day comes along.

"Sixth between Tenth and Eleventh," Tony said. "You two go ahead."

Nathan and Rose took the first cab the doorman flagged and paid a quarter for it. But the next was on the tail of the first, and they were stopped in order at Fifth Avenue. It was Rose who looked back from their leading cab.

"She's got it off already," she told Nathan. "She looks much better without it. Also, she's rubbing her forehead."

They arrived almost simultaneously at Charles French Restaurant. Tony Cook opened the door for them and Rose went in first. Rose said, "Goodness!" which is as mild a term as has ever been applied to the redecorated Charles.

"All the same," Tony said, "it's damn good food."

Which is also a mild comment on the kitchen of Charles French Restaurant.

Shapiro's In basket was full when he got to his desk at nine o'clock Monday morning. As he went through the squad room, Tony Cook was at his desk, typing. Detectives spend much time typing departmental English. Nathan Shapiro looked at his In basket, sighed and pulled papers out of it.

153

Fleming had sat in the lobby of the Hotel Algonquin until it was almost midnight and the lobby almost empty and the remaining waiter hovering. Subject, who had been described to Detective (1st gr.) Frederick Fleming had not reappeared. Fleming had gone out of the hotel to the car he had parked so he could see the hotel entrance. A few had gone into it; subject had not come out. Fleming had been relieved at eight in the morning by Detective (2nd gr.) Abram Cohen.

Cohen had gone into the restaurant of the hotel to have what was for him a late breakfast. He had found it an early one for the Hotel Algonquin guests. There had been only two other men having breakfast in the dining room. One of them, from description supplied, was subject. He was reading the menu when Cohen went to a table at a little distance. He asked the waiter something which Cohen could not overhear and the waiter shook his head. Subject looked annoyed, Cohen thought. No grits, probably, Nathan thought.

Cohen had finished his breakfast while subject was still drinking coffee. He had gone to the lobby and sat in it, partly behind a copy of the New York *Times*. Subject had come out of the restaurant and gone to the elevators and gone into one. Cohen had moved to another chair where the light was better, along with the view of the elevators. Cohen had waited half an hour, getting a third of the way through the New York *Times*. He had taken a chance and called in. He had been told to keep on waiting. He had not reported again at eight fifty-two.

Detective Alonzo Priory, attached to the District Attorney's Homicide Bureau, had got a photograph of John Henry Lacey III and wired it in. Copies were being made. Priory had not yet been able to see Leslie Sturdevant, senior partner of the law firm of Sturdevant, Grosvenor and Jones. He had, from this place and that, been able to sift out some information about Jo-An and John Henry.

Jo-An had not been especially popular in the area of Mobile, Alabama. It was too bad about her, of course—it sure was too bad about her. But that book of hers. Funny way for a Southern lady to be writing. Defaming the Southland, when you came right down to it. Writing like she was an outside agitator,

154

almost. One source had gone further. Way she wrote you'd think she was a nigger lover. Sho wouldn't have expected that from a daughter of John Henry Lacey II. You sho wouldn't.

There were fewer opinions about John Henry Lacey III. He was in the real estate business; Detective Priory had got the impression he was not very deeply in it. He was a member of the Plantation Club; all Laceys had always been members of the Plantation Club. Apparently he did not often visit the club. Stayed out at that plantation of theirs most of the time, seemed like. But he was a real Lacey, all right—not like that sister of his. Must be a problem to him, that sister of his. Probably the reason he didn't come into the city much. Embarrassing to have a sister who wrote books like that, defaming her own part of the country.

"Probably a member of the John Birch Society," Priory had reported to his bureau. "Hard to get people to talk about that. Could be he's a member of the K.K.K."

(Priory had added, not for the record, that he was the wrong man for this job; that it was a job for a WASP, which a man named Alonzo Priory obviously was not.)

The city police were cooperative; the sheriff's office was less so. Neither force knew anything against the Laceys. Except for that damn book of hers, of course. Sure was strange she should write like that. Fine old family, the Laceys were. You wouldn't expect a Lacey to do a thing like that.

Shapiro had read several chapters of *Snake Country* before he went to bed the night before. He had found them absorbing—an oddly moving picture of a land he could not imagine, but felt he was slowly coming to know as he read on; a country populated by black people and white people; a dozen characters of both races had become tangible in his mind before, at around midnight, Rose had called to him that he had better—had *really* better—come to bed. People he wanted very much to get to know better; people who grew in his imagination as he had waited for sleep. The heroine—at least he supposed she was going to be the heroine—had seemed to him to be a girl of subtle intelligence; a girl growing into a woman of discernment and of courage. And, he suspected, a woman who was to come to no good end. Jo-An herself, he had wondered. Jo-An as seen through Jo-An's now-for-always-blinded eyes?

Shapiro had not seen anything in the book which defamed anybody. But of course, Shapiro thought, I'm a product of Brooklyn and the son of a rabbi. I wouldn't know about products of the deep South, about sons and daughters of families who for generations had lived on plantations and once had owned slaves; men and women who looked backward while time ground them forward. I'm not, Nathan had thought before, finally, he went to sleep, even able to visualize what they call a "plantation."

The telephone rang on his desk. Detective Cohen had just called in, from a booth at Saks Fifth Avenue. Subject had got to Saks a little after nine forty-five. He had had to wait for Saks to open. Cohen had gone in after him, and into an almost empty store. After wandering around for a time, subject had gone to the shirt counter. Cohen was taking a chance in telephoning. But on the other hand, it was all chancy, with no crowd to merge into. Cohen had noted that he stuck out like a sore thumb and that he was chancing it and going to look at shirts himself.

So—John Henry Lacey III was stocking up on clothes. Possibly, recently acquired knowledge that he was his sister's sole legatee had sent him on a buying spree. The pertinence of this, if any, escaped Nathan Shapiro.

He used the telephone. Copies of the photograph of John Henry Lacey III had been distributed to detectives on the day shift. They were being shown to desk clerks and bellhops and waiters in hotels. This man? A week ago or perhaps ten days ago? If he had had breakfast at one of the hotels he might have asked for grits. Yeah, that's it. Grits. And damn if I know either, mister.

Shapiro looked at his watch. It was after ten. He got the Manhattan directory and looked up Oscar Karn, Inc. He dialed the number.

"Oscar Karn, Incorporated. Good morning."

Mr. Karn was not yet in; probably he would not be in until eleven or a little later. Yes, his secretary probably had arrived. "Who shall I tell Miss Prentice is calling?"

156

Shapiro told her who was calling. "One moment, please." A buzz. "Miss Prentice speaking. Can I help you?"

Shapiro told her how.

"I'm sorry," Miss Prentice said. "We don't expect Mr. Karn to be in today. As a matter of fact, he phoned to say he wouldn't be. That he had decided to extend his weekend by a day. Would you care to leave a message?"

"No message," Shapiro said. "But perhaps you can help me. It's my understanding your office received a manuscript from Miss Jo-An Lacey on Friday. The manuscript of her new novel."

"I believe that is correct. It came in late Friday afternoon, I understand. Special delivery, certified mail. Actually, I signed for it. And Mr. Karn called in and was told it had arrived. At least, I suppose it was the manuscript of her new novel."

"You didn't open it to find out?"

"Certainly not. It was addressed to Mr. Karn himself."

"We'd like to have a look at it."

"I'm afraid," Miss Prentice said, "that that would be quite impossible, Lieutenant. Without specific instructions from Mr. Karn, that is. And anyway—"

She paused for a moment.

"Anyway," Miss Prentice said, "Mr. Karn told me to have it sent up to him in the country. By messenger. And I'm quite sure the messenger has already left. If you'll wait a moment—"

Shapiro waited the moment, which turned out to be several minutes. He could hear the sound, but not the words, of Miss Prentice's voice, apparently on another telephone. Then she spoke again to him.

"The messenger left about fifteen minutes ago," she said. "By car. Or motorcycle, perhaps. Is there any other way I can help you, Lieutenant?"

There was no other way she could help Lieutenant Nathan Shapiro.

"He often takes manuscripts up to the country to read," Miss Prentice said. "Because there are fewer interruptions there, you know."

Shapiro said he saw and hung up. Almost at once the telephone blared at him. He spoke his name into it.

"Sergeant Finney, Lieutenant. At the bureau."

Which meant the D.A.'s Homicide Bureau.

Shapiro said, "Yes, Sergeant?"

"Detective Priory just called in. He's the man the lieutenant sent down to—"

"Yes, Sergeant."

"I don't know it was worth the long-distance toll," Sergeant Finney said. "Doesn't sound so hot to me, but the lieutenant said to pass it along to you. O.K.?"

"Yes, Sergeant."

"Seems this—wait a minute—this John Henry Lacey the Third is the girl's half brother. Father married twice, and John Henry comes from the first marriage. Al Priory just found that out this morning. Seems everybody down there had just assumed he knew because all of them knew. He said—I took this call of his—'They sort of figure, I guess, everybody in the world knows about the Laceys.' Also, he hasn't got to see somebody named—wait a minute—somebody named Sturdevant, because Sturdevant doesn't get to his office much before noon. And that the colored man at the plantation—only person there, Al says—is pretty vague about when Lacey left to go up north. Maybe a week, maybe two weeks. He can't rightly tell. Is pretty sure he'd have gone by train, or bus maybe, since the Laceys don't much like to fly, because that's the way the colonel and his wife got themselves killed. Al didn't explain that, Lieutenant. Figured he was running up toll charge, I guess. O.K.?"

"Probably their father and his wife," Shapiro said. "Her father and mother, that would be. His father. That's all Priory had?"

"Yeah. Not worth the charges, I wouldn't think. But the lieutenant said to pass it along."

"Yes," Shapiro said. "Pass everything along, Sergeant."

That John Henry and Jo-An Lacey were half siblings didn't, Nathan thought, looking at the cradled telephone, seem particularly important. Interesting, yes. Helping toward a solution? That was not evident. Would a half brother be more likely to kill for an inheritance than a full brother? That was by no means certain. Brothers kill sisters and sisters brothers.

Men and women too kill mates and their own children. Usually, of course, with guns and in the heat of family bitterness and despair. Jo-An Lacey had not been killed with a gun. She had been killed slowly and with deliberation. And almost surely, Shapiro thought, for money and not in rage.

Dejection grew in Nathan Shapiro's mind. He wasn't getting anywhere. More and more it was evident that this particular job was one for which he was outstandingly unsuited.

The telephone rang. At least I can answer telephones, Nathan thought, and picked the telephone up and said, "Shapiro." He added, "Homicide South," which was a waste of two words. To his own ears, his voice sounded grumpy.

"Terry Simms, Nate. Sound as if you'd got out of the wrong side of the bed. More than usual, I mean."

"Sorry, Terry," Shapiro said to Lieutenant Terence Simms, commanding the Detective Squad of the West Fifty-fourth Street station. "Maybe I did."

"Maybe this will cheer you up," Simms said, in a not-particularly hopeful tone. Nobody who knows him has much hope of cheering Nathan Shapiro up. "One of the boys has got a line on this man Lacey of yours. Thinks he has, anyway. Want to talk to him?"

"Yes," Shapiro said, and waited a moment and heard, "Detective Arthur Spencer, Lieutenant. Found a man who's pretty sure he waited on this man Lacey. At a hotel called the Brentwood. On Seventh Avenue. Run-of-the-mill sort of place. Identifies the photograph. Anyway, is pretty sure about it. Thinks he served breakfast to a man who looked like that in the coffee shop."

"When, Spencer?"

"Maybe a week ago. Maybe ten days ago. He's not sure. Like most of them, you know. Sort of remembers this man from the picture and sort of remembers he wanted something called grits with his eggs. Says he signed the check. Put his room number on it and signed. Only he signed something like Lawrence, the way he remembers it. Not Lacey."

"And?"

"A James Lawrence registered at the hotel on the sixteenth," Spencer said. "Sixteenth of this month. Checked out on the twenty-third. Was in Room Four-one-two. Nobody remembers anything about him and the pix didn't help. Except with this waiter."

"Bellhops?"

"One of them thinks maybe he took a suitcase up to Room Four-twelve about then. Doesn't remember the man. Not from the picture, I mean. Remembers taking a man—pretty sure just a man by himself—up to Four-twelve about then. Remembers, anyway, that whoever it was tipped him a dime and said, 'Here, boy,' when he gave it to him. The bellhop's around sixty."

"Black, Spencer?"

"Matter of fact, he is."

"From the sixteenth to the twenty-third," Shapiro said. "That's right, isn't it?"

"What they say."

"I suppose nobody remembers getting this Lawrence a cab when he left? The doorman? Or carrying his luggage down?"

"The Brentwood doesn't run to a doorman," Spencer said. "At a guess, most of their guests carry their own luggage. A check's out on the hackers, but you know how much time that takes."

Shapiro knew how much time it takes to check the trip records of taxicab drivers. He said, "Good going," and hung up.

It was good going. It was not firm; such things are seldom firm. If it ever came to picking John Henry Lacey III out of a lineup, the waiter from the Brentwood probably would say, "Maybe that one, I guess. Only I ain't sure."

Witnesses too often are like that. Witnesses tend to fade away.

The telephone rang again and Nathan said, "Shapiro," into it.

"Lieutenant Nathan Shapiro?"

"This is Shapiro."

"Long distance calling, sir. I have Lieutenant Shapiro on the line. You may go ahead, sir."

"This is Detective Priory, Lieutenant. Of the D.A.'s bureau. Detective Alonzo Priory. They said to call you direct if I had anything hot, only maybe this isn't all that hot. I'm calling from Mobile, Alabama, Lieutenant."

"I know where you are," Shapiro said. "Go ahead, Priory."

"About this Lacey kill, sir. Man named Karn involved in it. That's right, Lieutenant?"

"He's been her publisher," Shapiro said. "About Mr. Karn?"

"He was down here in April. Down here for about three weeks. At the hotel I'm calling from. He didn't stay at the Lacey Plantation. That's what everybody calls it. Plantation. But he had Miss Lacey here at the hotel with him. The whole three weeks, from what they tell me."

"With him? How much with him, Priory?"

"Not all that much," Priory said. "Different room. Different floor. He had a suite. She just had a room. From what I can find out, she was in his suite quite a lot. Seems, from what he more or less spread around, they were working together on a manuscript of hers. I sort of asked around about that, and it looks like they were, all right. Anyway, they had the public stenographer up several times. To his suite, I mean. They— mostly Miss Lacey but part of the time Karn—dictated to her. She said they had a lot of typewritten sheets with stuff written on them in pencil, and they would dictate from these sheets and say to mark it, 'Insert page two thirty-seven.' Or like that. And she would type it out with the page number. And Miss Lacey told her Mr. Karn was her editor and that he was suggesting some changes in her new book. The stenographer says she knew about Miss Lacey and that she wrote books. Seems she wrote one that made—well, quite a stir down here. The stenographer says she hasn't read it herself, but heard a lot of people talking about it. I don't know whether this is worth calling you about, sir, but the boss said to call you direct if I came across anything might be important."

"Yes," Shapiro said. "What we want you to do, Priory. Three weeks, you say?"

"April fifth to the twenty-fifth," Priory said. "Near enough three weeks."

"Near enough," Shapiro said. "Have you got to see this man Sturdevant yet? Her lawyer?"

"Last time I called he still hadn't come in to his office. You want me to call you after I've seen him, if I ever get to?"

"If she made a will," Shapiro said, "and he'll tell you what was in it, yes. No—only if the will doesn't leave her entire estate to her brother. If it does, just send your report through channels."

"Yes, sir. I'm calling from my room now, Lieutenant, and it will go on my bill. I'm supposing—"

"Yes, Priory. It'll go on your expense account. By the way, did you find out whether Mr. Karn paid for Miss Lacey's room as well as his own?"

"Yeah. I mean, he did, Lieutenant. Anything else?"

"What you can dig up," Shapiro said. "This Lacey Plantation is quite a way outside Mobile, I take it?"

"Thirty-two miles," Priory said. "If the rental people didn't rig their odometer. Sixty-four miles out and back was what the clock said. Only way to get out there, Lieutenant. Big sort of run-down place, but there's been work done on it. Recently, at a guess."

"Yes," Shapiro said. "This colored man you talked to out there. He couldn't be at all definite about when Mr. Lacey left to come north?"

"Week ago, he thought. Only maybe two weeks ago. Seems they take things sort of easy about time down here. Like getting into your office around noon. Could be it's the climate, I suppose."

Shapiro supposed it could be the climate. He hung up.

Detective Priory was doing a good job. Detective Spencer was doing a good job. So, apparently still at Saks Fifth Avenue, was Detective Cohen. Everybody's doing a good job, Nathan Shapiro thought. Except me, of course. I just sit and answer telephones. And pick up scraps and pieces.

That Oscar Karn had spent three weeks in Mobile in April, consulting with his author about her book, probably wasn't even a scrap. For all Shapiro knew, editors might often travel many miles to confer with authors. Authors who might produce best sellers, at any rate. Perhaps Jo-An Lacey had got stuck and sent out a call for help. He assumed that writ-

162

ers sometimes got stuck, like detectives. He hoped, for writers' sakes, not as irretrievably.

Three weeks in a hotel, and paying Jo-An's hotel bill. Not at Jo-An's house in the country. Understandable, that. The "plantation" was more than thirty miles out of town. Undoubtedly, Karn had flown down to Mobile and so would be without a car of his own—without, for example, the black Cadillac and the man named Stokes to drive it. A waste of time and energy to drive back and forth, of course. And with work being done on the house, Jo-An may not have had space for a guest.

There hadn't, obviously, been any secret about Karn and Jo-An having been at the hotel together; having worked together in Karn's suite; having called the public stenographer in to take notes and type inserts.

It was true that Karn hadn't mentioned being in Mobile during most of April. He had left the impression in Shapiro's mind, that he had, in recent years, seen Jo-An only in New York. But that, Shapiro thought, is only an impression in my mind, and impressions in my mind are worth their weight in smoke. I'll ask Karn about it when he shows up in town and Karn will say, "Sure, Lieutenant. There wasn't any secret about it. Sort of thing editors do all the time."

Separate rooms on different floors, Shapiro thought. More convenient if the rooms had been on the same floor, and only a door or two apart. But hotels cannot always give unlimited choice as to the locations of rooms they have available. If people want to visit one another in their rooms people must provide their own mobility.

A messenger refilled Lieutenant Shapiro's In basket. The Lucera case was due to come up in three days. Shapiro would have to testify. He made a note of that. The Hotel Algonquin would like to have release of the room formerly occupied by Miss Jo-An Lacey. Shapiro put "O.K. NS" on the request and put it in the Out basket. His copy of the photograph of John Henry Lacey III came through. It looked like Lacey, but probably was taken several years before. It showed Lacey, in jacket and nonmatching slacks, with his hand on the collar of an Irish setter. At least, the dog looked like an Irish set-

ter. Lacey looked at least five years younger in the picture than he had in the squad room of Homicide South and in the lobby of the Algonquin. He also, Shapiro thought, looked more robust. Also, he hadn't then worn a beard.

The telephone rang. I might as well be an answering service, Nathan thought, and told the telephone who was answering it.

"Detective Cohen, Lieutenant. I'm back at the Algonquin. Subject's still—hold it. I'd better call you back, sir. Looks like subject's checking out."

Shapiro said, "O.K., Cohen," and hung up. He waited about five minutes, and the telephone rang again. He said "Shapiro." It was not Detective Cohen.

"Weigand, Nate. This Lacey thing is heating up. The press is swarming all over Sully. So, Sully swarms all over me. So, consider yourself swarmed, Nate. The big bird pecks the littler bird."

"It's still a muddle, Bill," Shapiro said. "I told you I was the wrong—"

"You always do," Bill Weigand said. "Funny thing is, you never are. I'll tell Sully you're progressing. Right?"

"Sully" was Deputy Chief Inspector Dermit Sullivan, chief of detectives. The biggest bird in their part of the aviary.

"You'll have to, I guess," Shapiro said. "And he'll tell the press—tell them what, Bill?"

"That an arrest is expected," Bill Weigand said.

"You want me to come and fill you in?"

"If you like. It's still your baby. No, I'll talk to the inspector first. The less I know the better pitch I'll make, probably. Right?"

Weigand did not wait to be told that that was right. He hung up. He's a good guy to work for, Nathan thought. Too bad he keeps putting me on jobs I'm no good at.

The telephone rang. Shapiro picked it up and told it who he was.

"Cohen, Lieutenant. Sorry to have been so long. Subject did check out. Paid his bill and turned in his key. Bellhop took his suitcases out, and a big man in a black suit—chauffeur uniform but no cap—took the cases and put them in the trunk of

a black Caddy. Held the door of the Caddy open and subject got in."

"Subject being John Henry Lacey?" Shapiro said.

"Way he was described to me," Cohen said. "Tall thin man in a seersucker suit. Right? Only he isn't any more."

Shapiro said "Mmmm?"

"At Saks he was buying shirts," Cohen said. "You got that, sir? Paid cash and took them with him. I had to close in a bit, but I don't think he noticed. Then he went back to the elevators and took an express up. I figured if I went along he might get the idea he'd seen me somewhere before. The express elevator goes nonstop up to the floor where they sell men's clothing. So—well, I just waited around. Not much chance of losing him."

"No," Shapiro said. "Anyway, you didn't."

"Up there about half an hour," Cohen said. "Came down with a suit box. No shirt package, but probably that was inside with whatever he'd bought upstairs. So he went out on the Fiftieth Street side and got a cab and I got a break and got one myself. He went back to the Algonquin and went up to his room, and I waited around. Another half hour. Maybe forty-five minutes. Then a bellhop went up and came down with two suitcases and this man Lacey. Only, I damn near didn't recognize him."

He paused, presumably to let it sink in. Shapiro felt a little as if he were on a lead. He also felt a little annoyed. He said, "Why was that, Detective Cohen?"

"Well," Cohen said, "for one thing he'd shaved off that scraggly beard of his. Also, he wasn't wearing the seersucker any more. Gray slacks and a sports jacket. Gray and yellow, the sports jacket was. Sort of—well, snazzy. Didn't fit too well around the collar, but was all right. Wouldn't leave it for alterations, the way I figured. If he did buy it at Saks and it was what was in the suit box."

"It probably was," Shapiro said. "Drove away in a Cadillac, you say. With a chauffeur driving."

"Way it was, Lieutenant. Went off in style. Like—like a man who's come into money. That jacket—well, if he did buy it at Saks it must have set him back a bit. Two hundred, maybe.

Maybe more. Not that I run to clothes from Saks, but a friend of mine does. Damn good-looking jacket he had on."

Shapiro thought he detected envy in Cohen's voice. A detective's salary doesn't run to two-hundred-dollar sports jackets from Saks Fifth Avenue. Neither, of course, does the salary of a detective lieutenant, but Nathan Shapiro can always find more important things to worry about.

"I figured there was no point in trailing the Caddy in a cab," Cohen said. "Anyway, it had an out-of-city license number. A WP number. Which could be White Plains, I thought."

"You got the license number?"

"Sure." He gave it to Shapiro. It was the license number Shapiro had expected it would be. Shapiro said, "Good job, Cohen," and got "Thanks, Lieutenant. There's one other—"

He hesitated. Shapiro waited.

"This chauffeur," Cohen said. "The man who put Lacey's cases in the Caddy. I had a feeling I'd seen him somewhere before. Only—well, the feeling was pretty damn vague, you know what I mean. Just that he was sort of familiar and that I ought to be able to place him somewhere. Only I'm not. Maybe it will come to me."

"As a client, Cohen?"

"Could be. Doesn't have to be. I'm sorry, sir."

"No use trying to force it," Shapiro said. "The name Stokes help you any?"

Cohen repeated the name. He repeated it a second time. Then he said, "I can't say that it does, Lieutenant. Like I said, could be it'll come back to me."

With the telephone again in its cradle, Shapiro looked at it for several minutes. Then he used it to get Tony Cook at his desk in the squad room.

"I think," Shapiro said to Cook, "we're going to take a little ride into the country. Suppose you get a car set up."

"Sure," Tony said. "Right away."

"There's no great hurry," Shapiro said. "Half an hour will be about right. Give them a good head start, half an hour will."

166

14

The police car, which was not marked as a police car, loitered north. On the Saw Mill River Parkway it carefully adhered to the posted speed limit, which for most of the way is fifty miles per hour. As a result, it was passed by almost every other car headed north. Volkswagens were the most frequent passers. They were also the ones which most often hooted contemptuously. Tony Cook, who was driving, now and then hooted back, but he obeyed instructions, which were to take it easy.

The head start had been adequate. The black Cadillac was parked in the turnaround in front of Oscar Karn's big house. Passing it, Shapiro touched the hood. It was warm, not hot.

There was no sign of life around the Karn house. They walked toward the door, but, when still some feet from it, Shapiro stopped and turned. A clicking sound had come from the side of the house. After a few seconds there was another click.

"Somebody practicing his golf shots," Tony Cook said, stopping alongside Shapiro. Shapiro said it sounded like that, and they turned and walked on smooth turf, rounding the end of the house. There was a swimming pool there, with chaises around it. A gray-and-yellow sports jacket was stretched neatly over the back of one of the chaises. A little table beside the chaise had a glass on it. Green foliage seemed to be growing out of the glass.

John Henry Lacey III was beyond the pool. He swung a golf club, and a white ball rose from the grass and arched thirty feet or so through the air and came to rest in the grass. Lacey put another ball down and pulled his golf club back but then lowered it without hitting the waiting ball and turned to face Shapiro and Tony Cook.

He looked very different without the straggly beard. He looked, Nathan thought, much more like the man in the photograph. He needed only the red setter to be the man in the photograph. He wore a white polo shirt, buttoned nearly to the throat, and gray slacks. He looked at them for a moment and then, still carrying his golf club, walked toward them. He went around the swimming pool, and as he walked nearer his eyebrows went up slightly. He had, Shapiro noticed, had a haircut since the night before. When he was a few feet away, he stopped and let the golf club dangle.

"Well," Lacey said, "you two again."

There was not nearly so much of the deep South in his speech, Shapiro thought.

"Yes," Shapiro said, "it's us again, Mr. Lacey."

"If you want to see Karn," Lacey said, "he's not to be disturbed. Reading Sis's book. Shut up in what he calls his office. Everybody's supposed to go around on tiptoe. Only Mrs. Karn went off in her own car to play golf. Seems she's in a tournament."

He went over to the chaise and took his jacket off the back of it and put the jacket on. It didn't fit too well around the neck. Lacey pulled briefly at the lapels to tighten the collar and then sat down in the chaise. He lifted the glass from the table beside it, but put the glass down without drinking from it.

"Probably," Lacey said, "I could arrange to get you gentlemen a drink. Showed Mr. Karn's boy how to make a julep yesterday." He sipped from the glass. "Almost showed him, anyway."

It was warm in the sun, and it was a little after noon. The

168

ice-filled glass looked attractively cooling. Tony looked at it and turned his eyes away.

"I guess not, Mr. Lacey," Shapiro said. "One or two questions we'd like to ask you. Nothing you have to answer unless you want to."

"About Sis's death? I'll answer anything I can, Lieutenant—Shapiro."

He hesitated momentarily before he spoke Shapiro's name. It was as if he found the name difficult.

"Whyn't you sit down and ask your questions?"

Tony pulled up two director's chairs and they sat in them, facing Lacey, who didn't, now, look or speak so much like a caricature of the old Southern colonel. Before, he'd looked—Tony briefly searched his mind—before, he'd looked like somebody's picture on the label of a whisky bottle. "Colonel Culpepper's Rare Old Sourmash Bourbon."

"When you went around to Mr. Shepley's apartment the other day," Shapiro said. "The day your sister's body was found, he got the impression you'd just got to the city. Had gone down to your sister's apartment from the railroad station. Expecting to find her alive."

"That's right," Lacey said. "That's the way—"

But then he stopped and looked for some seconds at Shapiro. Again he raised inquiring eyebrows.

"But it wasn't that way, was it, Mr. Lacey?" Shapiro said. "And you don't have to answer that question. You don't have to answer any questions. You can get in touch with a lawyer if you want to."

"Warning me?" Lacey said. "In accordance with the rulings of that damn court of yours?"

"Just telling you you don't have to answer any questions you don't want to," Shapiro said. "You didn't just get into town that day, did you? Were in town a week before that. Stayed at a hotel called the Brentwood. Registered there as James Lawrence, not as Lacey."

"All right," Lacey said. "I did get to New York a week or so before Sis was killed, yes. And called myself Lawrence. Because—well, because I wanted to look around a little without advertising who I was. Because Sis was so well known and all."

"You said you got a letter from Mr. Karn on Tuesday, June twentieth," Shapiro said, "and that he had made a reservation for you at the Algonquin for the twenty-third. But in fact you were already in New York on the twentieth. How did you know about the reservation, Mr. Lacey?"

"Well, he did write me asking me to come up, I reckon a week sooner. And I thought I'd like to come up but, as I said, look around a little, so I told him—I telephoned him same day I got the letter—that I couldn't come for a week, and then he said he'd make that reservation for me for the twenty-third. But I left the same day too—traveled overnight on the train and got here the sixteenth. So I got his letter the fifteenth. Stayed at the Brentwood, like you said."

"Incidentally," Shapiro said, "Jo-An was your half sister, wasn't she? Not your full sister?"

"Sure," Lacey said. "Everybody knows that. In our part of the country, anyway."

Only up here in the North are ignorant natives uninformed about the Laceys. That seemed to be the implication. I'll never understand these people, Nathan thought.

"Does it make any difference?" Lacey asked.

"I can't see that it does," Shapiro said. "Just trying to get things straight in my own mind, Mr. Lacey. You came to New York the sixteenth?"

"That's right," Lacey said. "Went up the street a few blocks and found this hotel, which looked pretty much all right. Looked clean, anyway, and as if it wouldn't cost too much. Checked in. Decided, on the spur of the moment, that I might as well be James Lawrence. Knew a man named that once and the name just came into my head."

"You thought using your own name would—would what? Interfere with this looking around you wanted to do?"

"Yes. You may not understand this, Lieutenant, but it's hard for a Lacey to be—well, call it anonymous."

Neither Cook nor Nathan Shapiro made a direct response to this. Cook looked away from Lacey, and out over the swim-

170

ming pool. There was nothing to see there but gently rippling water.

"Looking around for what?" Shapiro said, after the pause.

"Well," Lacey said, "I'd got this letter and it worried me about Sis. So I decided to come up here and see if there was really anything wrong."

"What letter, Mr. Lacey? A letter from your sister?"

"She wrote me. Sure. Not the letter I mean. I mean the letter from Mr. Karn. Said he was worried about her state of mind. Thought I ought to know. He said he didn't seem to be getting through to her. Said she seemed to be depressed. So I came up."

"And?"

Lacey took a sip from his glass. He said, "I don't get you."

"What did you do about your sister, Mr. Lacey?"

"Went around to this apartment she'd rented to work in. Talked to her. Took her out to dinner. Thought I'd try to cheer her up."

"Did you think she needed cheering up? That she was depressed, as Mr. Karn had written you he thought she was?"

Lacey said, "Well." There was, Shapiro thought, some doubt in the word. He drank again from his tall glass with the mint sprouting out of it.

"When she was working it was—oh, hard to get through to her. It was sort of as if she wasn't there, if you know what I mean. I couldn't see she was much more that way than she usually was when she was doing this writing of hers. Abstracted. Sort of as if she was some place else. But that's the way she usually was when she was what she called working."

"But you didn't feel she was any more that way than usual? Regardless of what Mr. Karn thought."

"Just figured maybe he saw something I didn't. After all, he'd known her a long time and pretty well. Maybe better than I did. He's used to people like her. People who write books and that sort of thing."

"You felt Mr. Karn knew your sister pretty well," Shapiro said. "How well, Mr. Lacey?"

"You mean something by that?"

"Not necessarily. Your sister admired Mr. Karn. Was grateful to him? Because, from what he says, he pretty much discovered her as a writer."

"She thought he was pretty wonderful, I guess. Said things that made me think she did. Surprised me sometimes by what she said about him. Not the—well, not the sort of man people like us are apt to know very well, if you see what I mean. From up north and all. Different tradition, I guess you'd call it. Anyway, she was pretty sold on him, I guess."

"Stayed at the same hotel with him last April, as we understand it."

Lacey put his glass down hard on the table. He swung his legs over the side of the chaise as if he were about to get up. His face flushed.

"When they were working together on her manuscript," Shapiro said, without seeming aware of Lacey's movements or the look in Lacey's eyes.

Lacey didn't say anything for some seconds. Then he said, "Thought you were getting the wrong idea about Sis. Getting some dirty idea about her. About her and Oscar Karn. She was a lady, Shapiro."

The name seemed to come easier this time. But it also came more harshly.

"Mr. Lacey," Shapiro said, and now his own voice was harder, "we're not concerned about your late half sister's morals. We're concerned about who killed her. But incidentally, she wasn't a virgin. The autopsy showed that."

"Down where we come from," Lacey said, "we don't talk about our womenfolks being virgins. Or not being. You mean, they cut her up?"

"You can put it that way if you want to. There's always a post-mortem examination in the case of violent deaths. Do you know whether your sister had men friends?"

"Sure she did. What girl doesn't? She was just like any other pretty girl until this writing bug bit her. You trying to make out she was a tramp, Shapiro?"

"No. Now, you came to New York in response to Mr. Karn's

172

letter, apparently, and yet you didn't want him to know you were coming so soon. Why was that, Mr. Lacey?"

"I didn't want anyone to know."

"So you agreed he would make you a reservation at the Algonquin for the twenty-third of this month? The day your sister's body was found? That's what you told us, isn't it?"

"Yes."

"But you'd been in New York for some time before that. Staying at this other hotel."

"What I've just been telling you."

"Apparently," Shapiro said, "your sister was killed the night of the twenty-first. Had you seen her that day? Last Wednesday, that would be."

"No. You getting at something?"

"Trying to," Shapiro said. "You didn't see her last Wednesday?"

"I said I—wait a minute. I did call her up Wednesday. Along in the afternoon. Said I would take her out to supper. But she said she was tied up."

"Say how? Or with whom?"

"No. Just, 'I'm tied up. Call me tomorrow.' And I did, but nobody answered. You say she was—"

He didn't finish. Shapiro answered what he had not asked.

"Yes, Mr. Lacey," Shapiro said. "She was dead when you called Thursday. Did you call in the morning?"

"Yes. Pretty early, I guess. But she didn't answer."

"You weren't worried about her?"

"No reason to be I could see. I just supposed she'd gone out shopping or something. The way ladies do."

"You'd come up here to New York because you'd been told your sister was depressed. You couldn't get in touch with her by telephone. Did you make any other effort to find her?"

"Went down to this apartment of hers around lunchtime. Rang the doorbell and she didn't answer. But, hell, that had happened before. Sometimes she just didn't want to be bothered." Lacey leaned back in the chaise. "Back home she used to shut herself in her room sometimes. I'd hear her type-

173

writer going, mostly. Not always. But I'd knock on the door and she wouldn't answer."

"So you gave up trying to see her Thursday? You weren't afraid she'd—well, do something to herself? Being depressed, as you'd been told she was?"

"I told you she didn't seem all that down to me. Just—well, pretty much the way she usually was when she was working. Just not there, sort of."

"Did she ever mention—any of the times you saw her—that she was thinking of leaving Mr. Karn? Going to another publisher?"

Lacey sat up straight. "What're you talking about?" I've never seen him look surprised before, Shapiro thought.

"There was a rumor that she was thinking—"

Or seen him laugh, Shapiro thought. Lacey was laughing. "That's a mighty silly rumor," he said. "Though to tell you the truth, I never did know what she was thinking. But Mr. Karn has the book. He's reading it right now. Hell, I've signed an agreement—but that's none of your business, Shapiro."

"You signed an—" Shapiro said and stopped in midsentence. What stopped him was the opening of a french door onto the terrace of the house. The heavy-muscled man in a white jacket came through the door. He was carrying a tray, and the tray seemed somehow incongruous in his big hands.

He stopped on the terrace and looked at the three by the pool. He said, "Mr. Karn thought—" and stopped. Then he said, "I didn't know you had company, Mr. Lacey. Mr. Karn thought maybe you'd like something to eat, seeing he's still tied up."

Lacey looked at Nathan Shapiro and then at Tony Cook. He said, "I guess—" and let it hang.

"By all means bring Mr. Lacey his lunch," Shapiro said. "We'd like a word with Mr. Karn anyway."

Stokes came across the grass carrying the tray. He put the tray, which held sandwiches and what Shapiro took to be another mint julep, down on the table beside Lacey's chaise. He said, "There you are, Mr. Lacey."

"Mr. Karn," Shapiro said. He said it in a flat voice.

174

"Nope," Stokes said. "Mr. Karn's busy. He don't want to see nobody. Weren't you here yesterday, mister?"

"Yes, Stokes," Shapiro said, his tone suddenly mild. "I was here yesterday. And we're back today. And we want to see Mr. Karn."

He stood up. Tony Cook stood up, too. And Tony said, "Well, if it isn't my old friend Slugger Phipps. You haven't changed much, Phipps. Only I didn't expect to run into you as a waiter."

"You got something wrong, mister," Stokes said. "Never heard of nobody called Phipps."

"Assault with a deadly weapon, Phipps," Tony said. "Got away with simple assault because your mouthpiece argued your fists weren't deadly weapons. The man you beat up didn't agree, particularly. Hadn't come through with protection money. That was it, wasn't it, Phipps?"

"You're nuts, mister. My name's Stokes. Five years now I've worked for Mr. Karn."

"Since you got out," Cook said. "Mr. Karn know about that?" He turned to Shapiro, but kept his eyes on Stokes. "Seven years ago," he said to Shapiro. "I was in uniform. Cruise car up in the Bronx. My partner and I picked Phipps here up while he was beating hell out of a bookie who'd tried to hold out on the organization. Of course, the bookie happened to be a bit of a rat. But—sort of a little guy." He turned back to Stokes. "I'm not a little guy, Phipps," Tony Cook said. "The lieutenant and I want to see Mr. Karn."

"You're still nuts," Stokes said. "Whoever you are, you're nuts."

But it occurred to Nathan Shapiro that the man in the white jacket, which bulged so over his heavy muscles, spoke with considerably less conviction.

"That's right, Stokes," Shapiro said. "Detective Cook and I've come out from the city to see Mr. Karn. Suppose you tell him that."

There was a long moment when the three standing men looked at each other. John Henry Lacey remained on the chaise. He sipped from his new drink. It was, evidently, a situation in which Lacey had no intention of becoming involved. It was, however, a situation which did not seem greatly to surprise him.

Stokes broke first. He said, "Well, I guess I can go see."

He went off across the grass toward the terrace. Shapiro and Cook went after him. He went into the house and they went with him into the house. He went along a corridor and knocked at a closed door. There was at first no response. Then there was a scraping sound, as of a chair pushed along a wooden floor. There was the sound of feet on the wooden floor, and they sounded like stamping feet. The door opened and Oscar Karn glared at them. His beard appeared to bristle.

"I told you I didn't—" Karn said, and spoke loudly. But he did not finish that. He looked up at Shapiro. He said, in a slightly different voice, "What do you want now, Lieutenant? I helped you all I could yesterday."

"Perhaps not all you can," Shapiro said, and took a step toward the man in the doorway.

"No, Phipps," Tony Cook said behind Shapiro. "I wouldn't try anything. Way I told you, I'm not a little guy."

Shapiro did not look back to see what, if anything, Phipps-Stokes had been about to try. He went on toward Karn, and Karn stepped back into the room. Shapiro went into it after him, and Cook went along and shut the door behind them.

Karn's "office" was not a large room. It had a large desk in it, and papers were piled neatly on the desk. They were in two piles, the one which had been in front of Oscar Karn smaller than the other.

Karn went and sat at the desk. He said, "I'm working on Miss Lacey's manuscript, Lieutenant. But I'll help any way I can. I only hope—well, that it won't take too long."

"No, Mr. Karn," Shapiro said. "It shouldn't take too long. Is the book all you hoped it would be? Worth—say worth all the trouble you've gone to to get it?"

"Trouble?" Karn said. "I'm afraid I don't understand you, Lieutenant. What do you mean by trouble? Yes, it's a very good book. A very fine book, actually."

176

"A book that will sell as well as you hoped? As well as *Snake Country* sold?"

"I think so. In fact, I'm pretty—what are you getting at, Lieutenant?"

"Well," Shapiro said, "I'm a homicide man, Mr. Karn. I'm getting at murder."

"I know you think Jo-An was murdered," Karn said. There was dismissal, almost contempt, in his voice. "And that you can't find the murderer, if there was one. Anyway, I've told you all I know."

"Yes, Mr. Karn," Shapiro said. "We think Miss Lacey was murdered. But you're wrong in thinking we can't find the murderer. Because, you see, right now we're—"

They had their backs to the door of Karn's office. Both Shapiro and Cook whirled when the door banged open behind them. Shapiro's right hand started to move toward his shoulder holster, but the movement stopped.

Stokes's hands were just as big and powerful as ever. His left hand hung at his side. His right hand didn't. His right hand had an automatic pistol in it and the pistol was pointing. It moved, slowly, from Shapiro to Cook. Neither of them made a move toward his own gun after Shapiro's first aborted move.

"That's right," Stokes said. "Just be good boys. These gentlemen bothering you, Mr. Karn?"

Karn didn't answer directly. But he stood up behind his desk and began to move along it toward a french door which opened on the terrace. He reached it and, still facing into the room, reached behind him and raised the lever which dogged the door closed. He pushed back against the door and it swung open. Only then did he answer Stokes.

"I'm afraid they've got some absurd notion," he said. "Yes, Stokes, you could call it a bothersome notion. So—"

"Just stay where you are, boys," Stokes said and started to sidle toward Karn. He had to sidle around the desk and, for a moment, his back was to Tony Cook. The moment was long enough.

Tony kicked hard, and the toe of his heavy shoe caught

177

Stokes behind the right knee. Stokes staggered but did not fall. Tony reached out toward him, but Stokes escaped the reaching hands and turned on Tony with the automatic up and less than a foot from Tony's chest. "You son of—" Stokes said, and Nathan Shapiro's gun cracked, the sound enormous in the small room. The automatic flew out of Stokes's hand. There was blood on the gun when it clattered on the floor.

Stokes crouched, groping for the gun. Tony's fist crashed into his jaw, and Stokes reeled back and against the desk. He stood against it for a second and then, slowly, slid down against it to the floor.

Shapiro whirled. Karn wasn't in front of the french door. He was running across the terrace. He had pushed the door closed behind him, and Shapiro had to wrench it open. He went through it, his revolver ready, and Karn was running on the grass beside the house and toward the front of it and the police car standing there.

Shapiro yelled "*Stop!*" and Karn didn't stop. He was almost at the corner of the house when Shapiro brought his gun up and began slow pressure on the trigger.

There was the loud crack of a revolver, but it didn't come from the gun in Shapiro's hand. Karn staggered and fell to the grass. He slid along on the grass and seemed to be clutching at it.

John Henry Lacey III came around the corner of the house. He had a revolver in his right hand, pointed at Karn. He walked toward Karn and looked down at him, and then let the revolver sag so that it wasn't pointing at anything except the ground.

Shapiro went toward the two.

"Got him in the left foot," Lacey said. "Thought you wouldn't want him damaged too much." There was no appreciable trace of the South in his speech.

Karn rolled over and sat, swaying, on the grass, which had a streak of blood on it. He stared down at his feet. Then he looked up at Lacey.

"Double-crossing son of a bitch," he said, and his voice was high and shaking. He tried to reach down toward his shattered

178

foot and didn't make it and rolled over on the grass and lay on his side, looking up at Lacey. "Son of a—" he said, but the rest of the words wouldn't come. They were lost in a wordless cry.

"Shouldn't say a thing like that, Mr. Karn," Lacey said, and the Southern intonation, which seemed to come and go in his speech, was there again. "Bad thing to call a man down where I come from. And I'm not. I'm not a murderer, either. Down our way we don't hold with killing ladies."

Stokes came out from the office onto the terrace. He held his right hand in his left, and blood dripped from the hands. Tony Cook was behind Stokes. His revolver was jammed against Stokes's back.

"Looks like we'll need an ambulance, Lieutenant," Tony Cook said. He looked down at the man lying on the lawn. "Two of them, maybe?"

"Oh," Nathan Shapiro said, "I think we can get them both in one, Tony. After we patch them up a little. The stuff's in the car."

15

Rachel Farmer opened her apartment door quickly when Tony rang the doorbell at a few minutes after six on Tuesday evening. She was fully dressed, to Tony's mild surprise. The first thing she said was, "I thought it was the other one. The brother. For the money."

It had been in the newspapers all day; it had been on television the night before. The *Times* had given it a two-column front-page head Tuesday morning. (The lead story, right-hand column, had still to do with the common market.) The *News* had really splashed it. The *Post*, an afternoon paper which hits the street in the morning, had the arraignment, which was what was left and was not really a second-day story. It also had all the *News* had had and most of what had appeared in the *Times*. It didn't have so much about Oscar Karn's long and admired career as a publisher, but the *Times* book reporter had written that and had known his stuff.

Tony Cook removed his jacket and his shoulder holster with the gun in it. He said, "So did I, up pretty near to the end. But Nate didn't. Didn't like the idea of a brother killing a sister. Knows it happens but doesn't like it. And didn't think this Lacey was the type, anyway."

"The type to carry a gun, though," Rachel said, while Tony put drinks on the table in front of the sofa.

180

"Neither of us had figured on that," Tony said, and sat beside her. "Came as a nice surprise. Surprise to Karn and that thug of his, too. Only, not so nice a surprise to them."

He drank from his glass of bourbon on the rocks. Rachel sipped from her small glass of Tio Pepe. She has beautiful hands, Tony thought. He looked further. And beautiful legs, he added.

"Lacey said that down home everybody has a gun," Tony said. "I told him in New York it's against the law to have a handgun without a permit. He said that was a pretty crazy law."

"Bound over for the grand jury," Rachel said. "I read that much. Just so he could get to publish this book of Miss Lacey's? It doesn't seem very reasonable."

"Murder never is," Tony said. "Sometimes it seems reasonable to people. Did you read the *Times* this morning?"

"I don't read the *Times* much," Rachel told him. "It's too long."

"A piece about Karn," Tony said. "I mean, in addition to the news story. Kind of a profile. You didn't read that?"

She hadn't read that.

"Karn's been a publisher for a long time," Tony said. "Very big at it. Published a lot of stuff by people who're famous now. Famous or dead, of course. Discovered a lot of them. Made Karn, Incorporated, famous too. Only, the last few years, the corporation—Karn was the corporation apparently—began to dwindle down. Authors went to other publishers. Or just, as I said, died. Jo-An Lacey's big hit put Karn back on his feet for a while. Several years ago, that was. But he was left, toward the end, with nothing much to merge with."

She shook her head.

"He was planning to merge with another publisher," Tony said. "What it amounted to, probably, was that another publisher was going to buy him out. Only, he didn't have much to sell. Unless he could come up with another big hit. Like another Lacey best seller. And then, Miss Lacey said she was walking out on him. That she'd been to see an agent who would get her a much better contract."

"Couldn't Karn have just given her a better contract himself?"

"He might have offered," Tony said. "Probably did. Only—well, if you found out you'd been played for such a sucker, would you want to accept any kind of offer from the guy who'd played you? I wouldn't. We figure the better break she got from a new publisher, the madder she'd probably have been at Karn."

"So he got mad back and killed her?"

"Mad in a cold, careful sort of way," Tony said. "He had to get the book, don't forget. Planned it very carefully, we figure. We figure he knew he'd have to kill her as soon as she told him she'd seen Morton—the agent I mentioned. He'd know he was going to lose her. But he could expect a certain amount of time before another publisher made an offer, and the more nearly the book was finished, the better. So he played it cool. Not knowing he was in for a hell of a surprise."

"Which was?" said Rachel.

"The book was accepted in a week—Morton said that was unheard-of, or something. So then Karn had to kill Jo-An in a hurry. He'll deny everything, of course. And he's already hired one hell of a good lawyer."

"So maybe he'll get off?"

"Nate doesn't think so. The District Attorney's office doesn't think so. The jury'll have the last thought, of course. There's more. You want to hear what more there is?"

"Yes," Rachel said. "After another sherry, though."

Tony poured her another sherry from the chilled bottle. He freshened his own drink.

The way they figured it, Tony told her, Karn planned Jo-An's death to be thought a suicide. He wrote Lacey saying Jo-An was very depressed and that Lacey had better come up and see what he thought. He even made Lacey a hotel reservation. Planned the depression to explain suicide.

"And if we didn't buy suicide," Tony said, "Lacey would be on hand to be suspected. Since, after all, he was the obvious one who profited. He gets her money, and it's probably quite a lot of money. We're still checking that out. But we couldn't

D :

182

suspect him if he was nicely tucked away in Alabama. So—get him up here. He struck a snag there too, though—Lacey wasn't up here, as far as he knew, when he killed her. The reservation had been made for Friday, the twenty-third, and Jo-An was killed the night of the twenty-first. We can only guess why he didn't wait until the weekend. Jo-An's agreement with Morton was to take him the finished book and sign the contract Monday. That would have been yesterday."

"What's your guess?"

"Oh—we have two or three. Jo-An got this acceptance from Materson, the publisher, that same day, and from what Morton said about the contract, the terms were like nothing she'd ever seen before. She must have spilled the whole thing to Karn, and it's possible she got herself so worked up she told him she was going to march right to Morton and sign the contract the very next day. Not wait until Monday. Or she may have said she'd already signed the contract but was going to deliver the manuscript. Or—oh, some such thing made him decide he'd better not wait.

"So then he could only hope that we'd buy suicide. And, if we did buy suicide, get Lacey to sign this agreement."

"You leave things out," Rachel said. "What agreement? There wasn't anything in the papers about an agreement."

"Well," Tony said, "we don't have to tell the newspapers everything. Agreement between Karn and Lacey. Lacey as executor of his half sister's will. 'In consideration of five thousand dollars, receipt of which is hereby acknowledged, Lacey, as party of the first part and executor of the will of Jo-An Lacey, deceased—'"

"Would you just as soon put it in English, Tony?"

"In consideration of five thousand bucks, Lacey agrees to sign, as executor, a contract for the publication of a novel by Jo-An, presently titled 'Lonely Waters,' on terms to be mutually agreed. Lacey's signature notarized—Karn took him to some notary in Mount Kisco. Saturday. And gave him a first payment of five hundred in cash. With which Lacey went out Monday morning and bought himself some new clothes. He says it all seemed perfectly O.K. to him and that he didn't suspect Karn at any time until I spotted Stokes as an ex-con. Lacey said, 'That sort of made me wonder. Why'd a man like Karn want to have a thug around?'"

"Nate had wondered about that a good deal earlier," Tony said. "I suppose it was as much that as anything which made him settle on Karn."

Rachel shook her head. She said, "What thug, Tony? I didn't know there was a thug involved."

The "thug," he told her, was named either Stokes or Phipps —or, perhaps, neither. He was employed by Oscar Karn as chauffeur. "And apparently as bodyguard." And he had broken into the office of Phillips Morton, authors' agent, slugged Morton, who unexpectedly came in on a Sunday morning, and made off with an unsigned contract for the publication of Jo-An Lacey's new novel. A contract not with Oscar Karn, Inc.

Rachel shook her head again. She said, "Can this Mr. Morton identify him?"

"No. But you can be sure of things you can't prove," Tony told her. "Whoever slugged Morton was a big, muscular man. Nate noticed Stokes was that the first time he saw him, at Karn's house. Karn wanted to get his hands on the contract. He sent Stokes to get it. And, yes, they'll both deny it in court. Karn's already denied everything. He'll keep on denying everything. And, conceivably, the jury will believe him. We think it won't. The District Attorney's office thinks it won't. That it won't believe it was a coincidence that somebody broke into Morton's office and stole only an unsigned contract. Oh, and some odds and ends from Shepley's file."

Rachel shook her head once more. She said, in passing, that her neck was getting tired. Then she said, "Why would Karn want the contract if it wasn't signed? It wouldn't have any value if it wasn't signed."

"He had to know either way, I guess," Tony told her. "The answer depends on what Jo-An told him the night he killed her, and we'll never find out just what she said."

"Killed her and—and took the manuscript."

"Yes. Also the typewriter. What he did with that we don't know yet. Possibly drove over and dropped it in the North

River. The manuscript he wrapped up and mailed to his office—mailed it the next morning from the main post office on Eighth Avenue, we think. Wouldn't have risked a branch office, where he'd be more likely to be remembered. We're checking out on the clerks at the main post office who were on duty that morning; who would have weighed a pretty big package for first class postage. We may come up with somebody."

"About the contract," Rachel said. "If she had signed it, Karn would have lost the book. Even with her dead?"

"Yes. If the signature could be authenticated. If she had signed it, it would have been in the presence of Phillips Morton, as witness. All perfectly valid, and the other publisher would have got the book."

"And now Karn will get it? If he isn't convicted of murder?"

Tony shook his head. "Because," he said, "Lacey won't sign the contract. As executor of his sister's estate. And as the beneficiary under her will. All he's signed is a declaration of intent."

This time she nodded. But the nod was somewhat halfhearted. "Just because you and Nate guessed Stokes was the man who had stolen the contract," she said. There was still doubt in her voice. "But the lieutenant didn't recognize this Stokes or whatever when he saw him first. He—what? Just guessed?"

"We have to guess sometimes," Tony said. "Nate's good at guessing. And at putting two and two together. It was Karn or Lacey from the start. Both stood to profit. But Lacey, so far as we knew, didn't have a suitable ex-con in his employ. So—"

"So Mr. Shepley was just a red-bearded herring?"

Tony grinned at her, and emptied his glass.

"Shepley," he said, "was sort of what they call a catalyst. That is—"

"Mister, I can read and write. I'm not—well, I'm not just somebody to go to bed with."

"You're fine to go to bed with," Tony said. "Speaking of which—"

"Speaking of which, we're going to have dinner, aren't we? How a catalyst?"

"He got Jo-An to go to his literary agent. Who got her a contract. And told her how she'd been gypped. Where do we want to go to dinner?"

"The Algonquin. And I won't wear that damn wig. And after that, there's a movie uptown I'd like to see and—don't look at me like that, Tony Cook."

"I'm not looking at you any special way," Tony said. "If you want to go to a movie, we go to a movie. Only—"

She waited a moment. Then she said, "Only, dear?"

"Only," Tony said, "tomorrow I go on the four-to-midnight shift." He paused. "For a month," he added.

Rachel Farmer said, "Oh." Then she said, "I guess we can skip the movie, Tony."

He put a hand on the nearest pretty knee.

"But," Rachel said, "not dinner. We won't skip dinner, Tony."

He took his hand off her nearest knee. He poured them fresh drinks.